MW01115368

Not Myself

by Faith Miller

Deep Sea Publishing, LLC

This is a work of fiction. Names, characters, places, and incidents either are the product of the author's imagination or are used fictionally. Any resemblance to actual persons, living or dead, events or locales is entirely coincidental.

Deep Sea Publishing ISBN: 0983427682
Deep Sea Publishing ISBN-13: 978-0-983427681
Deep Sea Publishing E-Book ISBN-13: 978-0-983427698

www.deepseapublishing.com
Printed in the United States of America
eBook created in the United States of America

Table of Contents

Dedication

To my mom, dad and Andrew for always being so supportive of me, and to Hannah H. (Lana), Mary S. (Mandy), Michael T. (Ethan), Devin D. (DeLora/Lora), Amanda S. (Savanna), Garrett H. (Gabriel), Kylie M. (Nicole), Jessie D. (Jessie), Nathanael C. (Donny), and Amber C. (Clarissa) for being the people I could base my characters on. To Devin again for giving me an idea when I was at a big writer's block! To the many people who helped make this possible. And to my Lord and Savior Jesus Christ for saving me!

Chapter 1 - The Dream

I crouch into a ball in the corner. The pounding footsteps in the hall seem like thunder. My heart is beating so hard that I feel as if it might rip out of my chest if it doesn't stop first. My door opens and I see a shadow standing there blocking the light. He cracks his neck and inhales deeply. His lips curve up into a smile. He walks toward me.

"I'm thirsty," he rasps.

My muscles ache, as I am clenching my whole body. "Go away!" I scream. He keeps coming toward me and leans down centimeters away from my face. My throat is dry and it hurts to swallow. His tongue rubs over his upper teeth, revealing his fangs. He leans toward my neck but draws back. Is he second-guessing himself? Just when I think he is about to leave, he suddenly thrusts his face to my neck again. His teeth sink into my skin and searing pain rips through my body. I scream as I begin to dissolve away.

***

I wake up screaming and sit up in bed. My throat feels sore and raw, as if I've been screaming all night, which isn't hard to believe. My bed is damp from sweat and my heart is pounding so hard that my chest hurts. My eyes feel salty; I must have been crying in my sleep. I'm light-headed from breathing so hard. I touch my neck, half-expecting teeth marks, but of course, nothing is there. I turn to look at my clock and see it is two in the morning. I don't want to go back to sleep because every time I close my eyes, the man's evil face fills my mind. Soon, my breathing is finally back to normal. I go to the bathroom and drench myself in cold water to clear my head. I start to feel tired so I go back to my room and pull my blanket and sheets off. There is no way I'm going back to sleep in sweat-drenched sheets. I put new ones on and climb in. My head falls against the pillow and I fall back to sleep ever so slowly.

I do not dream again. My mind is blank when I try to think of what I had dreamt. It is probably best to keep my dream between me and my best friend. What if it means something? After all, that was no ordinary dream. As I get up and get dressed, I realize I am hungry.

My parents were not home last night. I don't want to think of where they were or what they might have been doing. My parents are continually getting drunk and often pull all-nighters. It's hard on me because sometimes I need them at home and I get really worried that they are going to get themselves in a car accident.

It all started after Dad lost his job a few years ago. They were both really stressed, went out to a bar, and just kept drinking. When they got home that night they could barely walk straight and were giggling loudly. It was almost scary for me, seeing my parents extremely drunk when I was thirteen, but they just went up to bed and slept for at least nine hours. Dad ended up getting a new job a couple months later, but by that time, they both enjoyed the feeling of being drunk so much that they just kept doing it, and I couldn't do anything to stop them.

***

I get dressed and walk quietly down the hallway from my room. My parent's bedroom door is closed so I am careful not to disturb them. They aren't mean to me when they are drunk, but when I wake them up, they are really cranky. Their hangover usually causes them to have severe headaches and sometimes they even start throwing up.

I heat up some waffles, eat, and walk to my bus stop. My best friend, Lana, comes up to me and immediately notices something is wrong. I tell her all about my dream.

"It's only a dream, Haley," she tells me.

That may be, but I can't help having a strange feeling that it is somehow more than that. I've never had such a dream that felt so real. Just then, I see Alex walking toward our stop. My knees start buckling because I have a major crush on Alex. Unfortunately, he has a girlfriend so we can only be friends. Even still, Alex and I talk a lot, and Lana tells me I blush when we do.

"Hey, guys!" Alex calls. A firework show starts inside of me as he walks toward us. His blue eyes brighten up when he sees me as he flips his beautiful black hair to the side.

"Hey, Alex!" I try to say as calmly as possible.

"Hey, did you get that Trig homework? I swear, some of those problems would've stumped Einstein!" he says.

"I know, I think some of them would qualify as torture in some countries!" I say trying to make him laugh. *He has such a beautiful laugh.*

Lana notices I am about to explode, and my cheeks are bursting with color. If something doesn't happen soon I might just lose my cool in front of him! Fortunately, the bus comes around the corner just in time. After we board the bus, Lana and I find a seat in the middle, while Alex sits with some of his other friends.

It really stinks that I have to take the bus to school. I can drive, but there are not enough parking spots at the school for the students. I guess it is off to another long day at school.

Chapter 2 - Alex

I trust Alex with pretty much everything, and I would do anything for him. I tell most people that he is like my brother just so it's not too obvious that I like him.

Later, I see him at school next to his girlfriend, Mandy, who is hugging all over him. I feel a surge of jealousy. I've seen leeches with more restraint. Mandy is really nice and she is so sweet, but sometimes, it is hard to be nice to her when I see her acting so possessive. She comes over to me.

"Hey, Haley! How are you?" she says.

"Good, how are you?" I say as cheerfully as I am able. I don't do a very good job at acting like I'm not mad at her.

"Is there something wrong?" she asks.

"Nah, I just had a weird nightmare last night and it's still kind of freaking me out," I say.

"Aw, well I hope you feel better!" She tosses her golden hair over her shoulder and turns to Alex. "Come on, sweetie. We'll be late for History class."

I roll my eyes and make my way to French class. After first period, Alex catches me in the hall.

"Hey, Mandy told me about your nightmare. Are you ok?" he asks.

I'm practically flying! I start to feel my face get hot. "Yeah, I'm okay. It was just a dream," I tell him. I'm a little embarrassed that I seem to be the kind of person who gets super afraid of nightmares.

Lana comes up to us.

"Hey, guys! What's up?" she says.

"Hi, Lana!" Alex replies.

I look at clock mounted on the wall in the hallway.

"Oh, shoot, guys!" I exclaim. "We only have one minute to get to second period!"

"Oh, crap! I'll see you guys later!" Alex calls.

"Later, Alex!" Lana and I shout to him. I turn to Lana.

"Your face is really red, Haley," she tells me. We laugh and head off to Physics.

After second period, Lana and I walk out of class into the hallway just in time to see Mandy grab Alex and kiss him. I take a deep breath, and we walk up to them.

"Hey, Haley! Lana!" Mandy calls.

"Hey!" I stink at acting! Mandy sees right through me.

"That dream still bothering you?" Mandy asks.

"Yeah, a little," I lie. The dream isn't really on my mind anymore. It is more on Alex.

Chapter 3 - First Sign

Because the Schedule Gods do not like me, I have no classes with Alex, so I don't get to see him until the end of the day on the bus. My heart speeds up to 100 beats a second when I see him. He's talking to his best friend, Donny, who is really cute but not as nice as Alex. At least he is not as nice to me. Lana has a slightly different opinion....

She and I sit down in the seat in front of them.

"Hey, guys. Donny and I were just discussing our English homework. We have to do a project on Hamlet. What was Shakespeare thinking? 'How do I bore high school students for the next six hundred years?' " Alex says.

I laugh. I think to myself, *I'm so much better for Alex than Mandy. I wish he could see that!* The bus starts moving. Our stop is the very first one, so we're off the bus in just a few minutes. I start off in one direction and Lana heads in the other.

"Haley!" Alex calls after me. I turn, and see he's running to catch up to me. "I thought I'd walk you home."

"You don't have to do that. I'm just at the top of the hill," I say, even though I really, really want him to walk me.

"I want to." I can't help from grinning though I do not understand exactly why he wants to walk with me. Best not to question it, I suppose. When we get to my house, I pull out my key and open the door.

"Bye, Alex," I say. "Thanks for walking with me."

"Later, Haley. Maybe you, me, Mandy, Lana, and Donny can all hang out tomorrow," he says.

"Yeah, we should!" I tell him. "I'll text Lana."

"Okay. I'll text Mandy and Donny and you with the deets," he says. I'm trying my best to stay cool, so I just nod and close the door. I run to my room and whip out my cell phone. I am just about to text Lana when I notice a neon Post-It note taped to my door. I pull it off and read it.

YOU ARE ONE OF US

Well that makes absolutely no sense. It's probably my dad playing a prank on me. Even though he gets drunk often, he is still a huge prankster. I crumple up the note, throw it away, and finish my text to Lana. I add in my text that Alex walked me home. Soon, I get a text from Alex.

"hey, how would it b if we go 2 c that new horror movie, ghostly fears?"

As much as I like scary movies, I don't want to see one since I just had a horrible nightmare last night. But at the same time I desperately want to hang out with all my friends. I don't want to disappoint them by saying "no" to a movie they are all dying to see. After texting Lana, I decide that I'll just have to risk having another nightmare. She tells me it looks like a really good movie and that we should all go to Denny's beforehand to grab a quick lunch. I text Alex and it's set. Unfortunately for me, I know that Mandy will be all over Alex during the movie because she's "scared." I guess I can't blame her because I would do the same thing.

I decide to go to the track because running is one of my favorite ways to relieve my stress and clear my mind for a while. I pack a bottle of water, my iPod, a hand towel, and my cell phone into my pink and green gym bag. Then, I drive down to the gym and head to the outdoor track. No one else is there. I love being on the track alone because I don't have to worry about anyone watching me "attempt" to exercise.

After I stretch, I start running. I've only run one lap when my legs start to tingle, so I stop, sit on the bench, and stretch some more for a couple minutes. When the tingling stops, I get up and try to run again. Soon, my legs are tingling again and I'm running fast-- make that faster than fast. The wind sounds in my ears, deafening me to all other noises. My hair is flying back in a model-like fashion. My feet start to get warm from the traction, but it doesn't matter to me. Even though this is the weirdest thing that has ever happened in my life, I can't help but enjoy the feeling of the wind blowing in my face, making me feel like a real runner.

After a full minute, I have run a little over a mile.

I grab my cell phone out of my bag and tell Lana to meet me at the track ASAP. She gets there in about five minutes. I tell her what happened and run around the track, but I can't repeat my speed. I meet Lana back at the same place.

"I swear! I was just like The Flash! You should've seen it!" I say.

"Haley, I'm your best friend, and as much as I want to believe you, you have to understand that it seems kind of far-fetched. But assuming you are telling the truth, I guess you just need to learn to control it. That's really all I can say."

What's happening to me? Why?

Chapter 4 - Hanging Out

I may trust Alex with everything, but this is one thing I know I should keep between me and Lana because if she didn't believe me, everyone else will definitely think I'm crazy. Lana offers to stay the night and keep me company since my parents will be out. I hope that whatever is going on with me doesn't affect tomorrow. I don't want to miss this hangout--even if Mandy is all over Alex because it is still a chance for me to be close to him. I drive home and Lana heads over to her house to get her stuff. I walk in the front door of the house and on into the kitchen. My parents are there...kissing. They are really passionate about each other, so they don't much care who sees them kissing. Maybe that is another reason why they drink: so they can be more passionate. I clear my throat and they stop. My dad leaves to go get his supplies for his class tonight.

"Hi, honey. How was your day?" my mother asks.

"Kinda strange, but overall pretty good."

"Oh? How was it strange?"

Oh, shoot! I couldn't tell them that I had suddenly become a speeding bullet and raced around the track at breakneck speed! "Just strange, I guess. Me, Lana, Alex, Alex's girlfriend, Mandy, and his friend, Donny are hanging out tomorrow. We are going to eat at

Denny's and see the movie, *Ghostly Fears,*" I explain, quickly trying to change the subject.

"That's great. Listen, I have to go to work and your father is going to his class. We are meeting up later and hanging out for a while," my mother tells me.

"Ok. I invited Lana over. She should be here any minute."

She doesn't hear me because she is already out the door. My parents will most likely get drunk tonight when they "meet up" and won't be back until morning.

My doorbell rings. Lana is here. I open the door and we go to my room and flop onto my bed.

"I'm so excited about tomorrow!" I tell Lana.

"I know! Me too! I can't believe Alex walked you home! I mean maybe he is starting to actually like you…" she laughs.

We talk about Alex until Lana changes the subject. I can tell she can't wait any longer.

"So, Haley, what do you think happened this afternoon?" she asks.

I honestly have no idea. I want to tell Alex and for him to tell me it's going to be okay, but I can't. I can't trust anyone but Lana. This secret is too big for me to keep between just us. I'm going to have a hard time keeping it quiet.

"My legs tingled and suddenly… I was running. Everything was blurry but somehow I could still tell where I was going," I explain.

Lana and I stare at the ceiling, thinking. I grab my remote and turn on my television because I can't take the awkward silence anymore. We watch a few episodes of *Ghost Adventures* before I grab the telephone and order a medium cheese pizza and some breadsticks from Pizza Hut. When it comes, I pay the delivery man and we sit down and eat until we are stuffed. After eating, we change into our pajamas and Lana gets on the mattress that I had put beside my bed, I get into my own bed, and we fall asleep instantly.

***

I wake up before Lana does; however, she hears me get out of bed and wakes up. My parents are in the bedroom, sleeping away their hangovers. We fix some bowls of cereal and talk about how to handle this afternoon. We're meeting at Denny's at 2:00 pm for lunch, and then the movie starts at 3:45pm.

I tell her that we shouldn't order too much, or everyone will think we are pigs. And I can't have Alex thinking that! I pick up my bowl and put it in the sink. I then go to put on my favorite shirt and skirt combination and Lana gets dressed as well. We talk about Alex, school, stress, and all the other things a typical high school teenager deals with while I curl her hair and she straightens mine. This takes us a few hours because I have very long, thick hair that takes a long time to straighten. After we decide that we finally look decent, we go into the living room and watch TV until it is time to leave.

At 1:30, Lana gets into her car, I get into my own, and we drive to Denny's. Alex and Mandy are already there. When I step inside, I see Donny pulling into the parking lot. We see Alex and Mandy waving to us from a table, so we head over.

"Have you guys ordered yet?" I ask.

"Nope! We wanted to wait for the rest of you to show up," Mandy says.

Donny comes in and we all wave to him. Our waitress comes over and asks us what we would like to drink. Alex tells her we already know what we want to eat as well so he orders iced tea and French toast with eggs. Mandy orders Dr. Pepper and the combo meal of eggs, sausage, and bacon. I order milk and two pancakes with a side of sausage, Lana orders Coke and a cheeseburger with fries, and Donny orders water and a veggie burger. Lana makes conversation to get the ball rolling. We talk about school, a church mission trip coming up, and reviews of *Ghostly Fears* that we've either heard from friends or read over the Internet. When our food arrives I try to eat slowly to keep from embarrassing myself. Just another joy that comes with being a "girl in love!"

After each of us has eaten all our food, I suddenly feel nauseous and I don't understand why. I couldn't have eaten too much or too fast, yet I have never felt this nauseous in my entire life! I walk casually to the bathroom so Alex doesn't suspect anything. I look in the mirror and notice that my face is very pale. I run into the stall and before I know it, I am on my knees vomiting into the toilet. I end up puking up my whole lunch. After a few minutes, I am finally done. I'm not nauseous anymore, nor am I even hungry. Thankfully, I managed not to get any puke on my shirt. How embarrassing would it be for Alex to see that?

My mouth tastes awful. I go to the sink and rinse my face off. As I walk back out of the bathroom, I glance over to our table where I see Alex and Mandy sharing a milkshake. I roll my eyes. It seems like I keep catching them together at the worst of times! I guess I didn't do such a good job of waiting for the color to return to me face because Mandy sees me and runs up to me.

"Oh, my gosh! Are you alright?" she asks in an almost frenzied voice, her bright green eyes showing genuine concern.

"Yeah, I'm okay," I say. "My stomach was just a little upset." *A little? I feel like I just threw up a car!*

"Are you sure you still want to go to the movie?"

"Yes, I'm fine," I tell her.

"Do you think it's connected to what supposedly happened with your legs?" Lana asks me as we walk to our cars.

"I don't know, but I don't understand why this is happening to me," I tell her.

I see Alex and Mandy get into Alex's car, and I can't help wishing that was me. We make it to the movie theater and meet up at one of the kiosks. Alex enters in all the information and we each pay for our ticket. We all buy popcorn and drinks and Mandy and Alex get some Twizzlers to share. Then we go find some seats.

The movie starts and I start to munch on some popcorn. After about 45 minutes into the movie, I start to feel nauseous again. I walk out and then walk faster to the bathroom. I run into a stall and the insides of my stomach start coming out again. I don't puke as much though because I didn't eat as much. I'm done in just a few seconds.

I walk back to the theater, frustrated that this is the second time this has happened in just a couple of hours.

"What'd I miss?" I whisper to Lana.

"Not much. All that happened is the girl heard a voice, but she doesn't know what to make of it," she explains.

I'm fine for the rest of the movie. Afterward, I drive home and Lana drives to my house to pick up her things.

First, weird things happen to my legs and now my stomach. What's going to be next?

Chapter 5 - Why I Can't Keep Anything Down

I am absolutely starving, but nothing is staying down. I don't know what is happening to me, but there has got to be something I can eat that won't make me sick. I go to my cupboard and search for something that won't upset my stomach. Mom taught me that the best thing to eat when you are sick is chicken noodle soup. Luckily, we have a can of that. I grab it and start to open it; however, when I pull off the lid, the sharp edge slices my finger and it starts to bleed. I wince and suck on it. If all that food made me sick, I'm probably going to get sick from this. That is when I realize my blood doesn't taste salty or like iron--it tastes...sweet, like sugar or honey. I quickly draw away. I wait about forty-five minutes, but I don't get sick at all. I don't even feel nauseous and that scares me.

I run to my room and slam the door and lean against it. I just want a regular high school life, with a crush on that one boy who I believe belongs with me. I want parents who are actually around most of the time. Not this—this change that's come over me!

I am still hungry, so I decide to cook that soup. It's very good, but it doesn't stay down either. Blood is the only thing that—I don't know—tastes "right." I shudder when I think about sucking blood, but my stomach starts to growl as if it's anticipating it. *Blood...where can I find blood?* I guess I am not going to find it staying in the house. I put on an old shirt I use for painting and tie my hair back into a messy bun. I go out to my car and start driving. *Where do I possibly find blood? A blood bank... a hospital...a butcher?* Ugh, that last one.... As I drive, I go by the woods next to the school. Then a thought comes to mind. *What about blood from an animal?*

It's really the only way to successfully get blood for me to drink without asking anyone and with a lower chance of anyone seeing me do so. I get out and start searching an animal to satisfy my blood addiction. I have never been so hungry. After walking for a couple minutes, seeking an animal in an almost frenzied manner, I come across a small rabbit. I stare at it, imagining what its blood must taste like and how good it would be to finally eat something that doesn't make me sick. My mind races as I try to decide whether or not I want to kill something so cute. I might as well get used to it since I'm going to have to do it for the rest of my life. The rabbit looks up at me with a strange curiosity in his eyes, not even thinking that the next few minutes are his last. I feel a surge of energy course through me, almost anger, and my legs tingle as I look at it and then move extremely fast toward it. This makes me wonder if these sudden bursts of speed have to do with an adrenaline rush or stress. But before I know it, the rabbit is in my hand. It's squirming, but I hold it up to my mouth and plunge my teeth into its neck, and start sucking. I close my eyes as the sweet taste of honey washes over my tongue and down my throat. Rabbit's blood is not as good as human blood, but it still tastes good. Since I've never bitten into an animal's neck before, this is a totally different and strange experience for me.

As I drink, I start to feel revived. My thoughts are scrambled between what has happened today, what I am doing at this very moment, and the one conclusion that is inescapable. *I am a vampire.* It's the only thing that makes sense. Only a vampire could be revived by drinking blood and have superhuman powers.

Vampire legends universally include fangs for sucking blood, but I do not have them, nor do I even know how to acquire such a thing. I need to figure out if fangs appear naturally or if there is another way to get them to grow.

There is no more blood left in the rabbit--not a single drop. It looks grotesque. He looks very thin, like a wet piece of torn clothing. I wipe my mouth off and realize my old painting shirt is very bloody. I'm glad I put it on.

Eating is quite messy without fangs, so I think I'll just take a knife with me next time.

For the first time today since lunch, I have had my fill and it's staying down.

I know that I won't be as lucky with getting my other meals, so I decide to set up a trap to capture animals. I take the rabbit I've just eaten, so I can use it as bait in the trap.

I drive back to the pet store and buy two animal traps to catch my food, which eats up almost all of my savings! There are cages where the door closes after the animal enters. The holes in the cage are large enough for me to stick a knife in and kill this animal without it harming me. I feel bad that I have to kill animals to get my food, but I can't kill people.

I drive back to the woods and set up the traps in a location that I know I will remember and place little bits of the rabbit and a small amount of rabbit food I bought at the pet store into each trap. The only thing I will need to do after I catch an animal is to take a knife and stab the animal until its dead. Then I can take it out and drink its blood.

I wonder if I should tell Lana about all of this. I tell her everything, but will she avoid me if I tell her this? What if it scares her and she doesn't want to be my friend anymore? How would I even explain this whole change to her and get her to believe me? Lana and I have been best friends for years, and I have to tell someone. I'd like it to be her. I go to my car and call her.

"Lana, we need to talk. Meet me at my house as quick as you can."

"I'm there," she says. I drive back and meet Lana in 10 minutes.

"Come on. We have to go to my room. I don't want to say it where someone might be listening," I say. When we are inside, I add, "Please tell me that whatever you hear, you will still be my best friend and will help me through this. And you can't repeat this to anyone."

"No matter what, I will always be there to help you, even if no one else is."

We sit on my bed, and I tell her everything that happened to me. Talking quietly, I start by telling her that I think there's an explanation as to what has been going on lately. But I don't say that I'm a vampire just yet. She's not exactly ready for that part…and I don't think I am either. I finish by explaining how I can only drink blood since it is the only thing that stays down, and how the blood tastes sweet to me.

Lana doesn't say anything. She just has a look on her face that says this whole story grosses her out immensely.

"You always were a good storyteller," she says trying to laugh. She obviously doesn't believe me. She may not want to.

"I'm telling you the truth. This whole change started with my legs at the track. The reason I was getting sick was because my stomach needs blood, not human food. I don't know how this happened to me or why and I don't know if I ever will. But you have to believe me. I don't think I have anyone else I can go to with this."

"You never proved the whole 'speed' situation to me. And maybe you just had something bad to eat and that's why you got sick."

I get up off the bed. "You really don't believe me. You're my best friend. I wouldn't lie to you about something like this."

I can feel my eyes start to water. I'm trying so hard to get her to believe me, but I don't know what else I can say.

Lana sighs. "You are telling the truth, aren't you? Usually, you just start laughing after the joke is over. But obviously, that's not the case."

"I just need one person to believe me, and you're the only one I can trust. I can't even trust my own parents."

"Well, you know what you are, don't you?" she asks. Of course I do, but I haven't said it aloud yet.

"I'm a freak," I say, my voice cracking slightly.

"No," Lana answers. "You're my best friend. I'm sorry I didn't believe you, but even you have to admit, this is really hard to process."

"I just can't believe it. I'm a......vampire," I whisper. This is the first time I have actually admitted this out loud; the first time it's actually real. The room is so quiet, my head pounds. Lana squeezes my shoulder as we look out the window, unable to say anything more to each other.

Chapter 6 - Flashbacks

Lana stays with me for the rest of the day and night so I have company. I can still sleep, thankfully. I guess the other supposed vampire trait of sleeplessness hasn't come in yet. Maybe there is no such thing as vampires not being able to sleep. After all, you can't believe everything you see on *Teenage Vamps*.

"Lana," I say in the morning. "I'm going to take a drive and get something to eat. Stay here and eat whatever you want."

"Okay, I'll just go see what you have in the kitchen."

I take a very sharp knife out of the drawer in the kitchen to take with me. I get in my car, and drive to the woods. Then I open my trunk and put on the same old "feeding" shirt I did yesterday. It's now covered in dark, red stains. I tie my hair back to keep it out of my face when I'm eating. After finding the trap I've set out, I'm delighted to see that there is an opossum that crawled in during the night. I take out my knife and stab the opossum through a hole in the cage. It hisses at me, but it is soon dead. I manage to forget about how disgusting opossums really are, open the cage, and drink the blood from the entry wound. It goes down my throat so wonderfully. After I finish drying this animal out, I take my knife and cut out little pieces of meat as bait for my next animal. Then I go to check my other trap and find it is empty. I'm disappointed because I'm still a little hungry, but I can only wait until the trap is filled. When I get home, I find Lana eating a muffin in the dining room.

"How did it go?" she asks as I enter the room.

"Awesome! I had possum for breakfast," I reply.

"That's disgusting!" she laughs.

"Trust me, it was!"

We both start laughing. "I'm going to go get dressed," I say. After all, it's probably weird for her to see her best friend wearing a shirt covered in animal blood.

I walk into my room, when all of a sudden; I'm not in my room anymore. My vision blurs and I'm flashed back to a time when I was thirteen. My father is talking to me.

"Hey, we need to have a talk," he says. A horrified look comes across my face.

"Oh, no, Dad! I've already learned about this from Mom!" I exclaim.

He laughs. "No, it's about something much more important. Around the time you're a junior in high school, you're going to go through some really, well, different changes…"

My cell phone vibrates and I get a text from Aiden, who was my boyfriend at that time.

I turn to my dad. "Hey, can we finish this later?" And then I go back to talking on the phone. He sighs and leaves the room. Dad was trying to tell me about what is happening to me now. Why hadn't I listened to him? Why had Aiden been so much more important? Would things be different now if I had just listened? How did he even know I was going to change?

My vision goes black and Lana is shaking me awake.

"Haley, Haley, are you alright? Haley, can you hear me?" she's asking in a frantic voice. I stir and stare up at the purple ceiling of my room until my mind registers what I just saw.

I realize I have fallen to the floor and I have a slight headache from my head banging on the floor, "Lana, I just..." I can barely finish. It seems too impossible to be true.

"I know. You just passed out," she says. "You could hear your head hitting the floor a mile away."

"No. I just saw something from my past that I didn't remember until now. My dad..." I falter.

"Your dad what?" Lana urges softly.

"My dad knows all about me."

Chapter 7 - Mandy and Alex

I don't go to school on Monday because I don't think I am ready to deal with this huge new change in my life at home, much less at school. My parents sleep all day, fighting off the past night's drunkenness, so skipping school is really easy.

On Tuesday, I decide that I have to go back to school. Missing too much makes people ask questions. Maybe Alex can help me get my mind off all this weird stuff happening to me.

I get an empty water bottle and fill it with blood from an animal in my trap. I bury it deep into my backpack, so no one will be able to see it. I plan to keep it hidden in my locker, then take a break before lunch and drink it. Luckily, I usually have a 10-minute break before lunch in my Study Hall class which should be enough time to fill myself up and then I can just go straight to the lunch room from there.

Lana and I meet at the bus stop. Alex starts walking toward us.

"Are you ok, Haley?" he asks. "After what happened last weekend, and when I didn't see you yesterday, I was worried."

He was worried about me? I smile sweetly. "Yeah, I'm alright. Lana and I got everything figured out," I tell him.

I can tell he has no idea what I am talking about, and he probably never will. The bus comes around the corner. We get on and Alex goes toward the back with all his friends. I wish I was popular like he. When we get to school, Mandy pulls Alex into a hug. She waves to me and walks with Alex to their History class. I groan and head to French.

At one point during the day, I see Alex talking with Mandy and she looks pretty upset. I shrug and head to Study Hall. After all, it's probably none of my business anyway.

When our break comes, I go to my locker, hide my bottle inside my jacket, and head to the bathroom. Then I go into a stall, take out my bottle, and drink it all. The warm liquid washes down my throat until I've had my fill. I wait until no one is left in the bathroom before I come out of my stall. My mouth is red from the blood. I wash it off, rinse the bottle out, and head to the cafeteria.

Lana catches up with me in the hall.

"How'd it go with, uh, you know?" she asks.

I sigh. "It was fine. It's just frustrating that I have to do this and can't eat in the cafeteria like everyone else."

I find us a seat in the lunchroom while Lana buys her food in the line. The aroma from the chicken and pizza is intoxicating. I want some so badly, but I know I can't have any. I'll just end up throwing it up anyway. Lana sits down beside me with fries and chicken tenders heaped onto her tray. She looks like she feels guilty. If she really felt guilty, she wouldn't have gotten so much to eat right in front of me.

"Lana, please. Let me just have a tiny bite of your food," I plead. "It smells so good and I just have to have some!"

"No! You know what will happen!" she says. I don't care. I grab a fry before Lana can stop me and I eat it. It tastes awful! Worse than my mom's cooking, and that's saying something! I grab a napkin and spit it out.

"That was repulsive! I've never tasted anything that horrible before!" I exclaim.

Lana tries a fry.

"They taste the same as they usually do," she says.

"It's because of you-know-what!" I say very frustrated. "I can't even have a bite of real food! Why does food taste so disgusting all of a sudden?"

"Maybe it's so that you don't eat any real food and make yourself sick. Your body must be trying to adjust. Like you said yourself, your stomach's made for blood, not food."

Alex comes and sits down next to me with Mandy alongside him.

"Aren't you hungry?" he asks me.

"I—" I try to search for an excuse quickly in my mind. "I had a big breakfast."

At the end of the day, I don't see Lana at all, so I get on the bus and see Alex with his head resting against the window. He is alone. I wonder where Donny is. I sit next to him on the seat.

"Alex, are you alright?" I ask gently. He turns to me. He looks extremely upset. I've never seen him this sad before.

"Mandy and I broke up," he tells me.

I'm sad, but happy at the same time. I can't let Alex know that, and I feel guilty for feeling that way. I don't want him to be sad, but now he is finally "dateable"!

"Oh, my gosh, Alex! I'm so sorry. You guys really liked each other," I say. It's really all I can say so that I'm not lying to him. I hug him. My heart reaches up to a speed I didn't know it could reach! My cheeks start to get hot. I know I am being selfish, but I have wanted him to be single for so long.

Lana gets on the bus with Donny. Donny sends me an invisible message through his eyes that tells me he knows what happened and needs to sit with Alex, so I give Alex another small hug and go sit down with Lana. I then tell her what happened. When we get off the bus, I tell Alex I hope he's okay and walk home.

Chapter 8 - The Visitor

So many thoughts surround my head. Mostly, I keep thinking about how Alex and I should date now that he is single. *But would that be wrong? I mean, if he just got out of a relationship, is it too soon to start one now? We are really great friends, but I want to be more than "just friends".*

I sigh deeply as I pull my key out of my backpack. I trudge up the stairs to my room and drop my stuff on the floor only to realize I am hungry. I decide to go into the woods and search for an animal to relieve my craving. The fresh air in the woods might help clear my mind a little bit. So put an old shirt on, tie my hair back, drive to the woods, find an animal, drink the blood, and drive home. I pause in the driveway. So much has happened to me in these last few days. I feel like I'm on a huge roller coaster with tons of ups and downs and loops and I can't get off.

Suddenly, I remember that note I found on my door a couple of weeks ago. I don't think it was my dad who put it on the door. It didn't look like his handwriting, but what could it possibly mean that I'm one of them? Who is "them?"

I get out of my car and run up to my room hoping that the note is still lying in my trash can so I can look at it more closely. When I reach my door, I get the feeling like I shouldn't go in. I don't know why, but I just have a tingling down my spine that tells me not to enter my room. Nevertheless, I slowly walk in and find that there is someone standing in my room. I can only make out a black figure. I really wish I hadn't come in here.

"You are one of us," the figure rasps.

Was this person the one who left the note? "I'm just me. A regular girl," I say shakily. I can't be too careful. What if he isn't?

The figure lunges toward me and pins me up against my now closed door. It hurts a great deal. *If I am one of their kind, why is this person treating me so roughly?* I see the figure pull some cloth out of its pocket. Even though I know the house is empty, I try to scream for someone, anyone, but it's quickly muffled. The sharp smell of chloroform fills my senses. I struggle and try to pull the cloth off my mouth before I pass out, but the hands holding it are much stronger than mine. My head starts to feel foggy and my vision blurs. I suddenly feel weak and cannot find the power to struggle anymore. I go limp and slip silently into unconsciousness.

***

I stir awake. My whole body feels like lead and my head slightly hurts. Suddenly, the events of what happened in my room come back to me. I realize I can't move! My hands have been tied behind me and my legs are bound with rope. *What did that man do to me?*

I try to break the ropes, but they are knotted so tightly that it is impossible. My heart is beating very fast. I see the door open and a man enters. He kneels down next to me. It looks like he doesn't want to hurt me which doesn't make sense. He already kidnapped me and in the movies, it always gets worse from there. He shows me a crumpled piece of neon paper. Then, he unfolds it. It's the note that was on my door last week.

"You passed my note right off!" he yells. I'm shaking violently out of fear. I try hard to not let him know I am afraid. It makes me more vulnerable.

"How could you just throw it away like that? You truly are one of us! I've been watching you. I know all about you and so does **she**," he explains. *Who is... she?* Despite my question, I'm too afraid to ask it. A frustrated look comes across his face. *Does he really want me to talk?* He actually strikes me across my face and leaves.

My vision blurs for a few seconds from the strike, and my cheek begins to throb.

"Help!! Somebody please help me!!" I cry out as I struggle against the bindings. No matter what I try, the ropes won't break.

The door opens again. The same man enters but with another man this time. They both kneel down next to me. I notice a bat fly in behind them, but they don't. The bat disappears behind the man on the right.

"You're hungry, aren't you? I can tell," the man on the left taunts. He's trying to torture me, knowing that my hunger will never be satisfied. I don't move. I refuse to give him the satisfaction of seeing me in pain. Suddenly, a man in his early twenties materializes behind the other two men. He grabs them from behind and slams their heads together. They stagger a little bit, then turn around and start throwing punches and kicks. But the bat-man dodges them all. He then punches them both in the stomach and they double over in pain. Then, the man hits them roughly on their backs. He comes to me and unties the ropes.

"Come on, we don't have any time to waste," he says. He extends his hand toward me, but I don't take it. "Haley, you can trust me." Though I don't know how he knows my name, I feel somehow comforted by his words and decide to take his hand. He starts to lead me out of this awful prison.

"I don't know where we are!"

"Don't worry! I do!"

Who is this man?

Chapter 9 - Almost Out

We keep running--going through all sorts of twists and turns in very narrow hallways. An alarm suddenly sounds, blaring in my ears. The two men who had taken me must have triggered it to keep us from escaping.

In hardly any time at all, we are surrounded by men, all of them obviously vampires. Their fangs are showing as they growl and hiss at us.

"Haley, run! I'll fight them off!" the bat-man yells at me.

Because I hesitate for too long, he pushes me through the circle of vampires and then turns to take them on one at a time. By the time he's done, all the men have either been knocked unconscious or are in so much pain that they can't fight back. I can only imagine how many years of practice it must have taken to get to his level of fighting.

Then he reaches for my hand and once again we start running to escape the building.

"Who are you?" I ask as we finally make it out of the strange building.

"I am a protector sent by someone close to you. I swore to protect you from any harm that came your way. I was the one who sent you the vision of your father telling you about your coming-of-age. I also tried to give you the feeling that you shouldn't go into your bedroom, but you disregarded it."

A guilty look comes across my face.

"It's alright now. I must do my job whether or not you choose to listen to me."

"How were you able to do that stuff to me? And how are you able to turn into a bat?"

"They are both special abilities given to protectors."

"So you protect me from anyone and anything?"

"Well, he did not know that I cannot protect you from **her**. That is your own battle."

"Who sent you? And who is… 'her'?"

"You must find that out for yourself. There are certain things I am forbidden to get involved in. I'll always be around in case you need my assistance or protection, but I am powerless to defend you against **her**."

More questions fill my brain than before.

We start running again to put some distance between us and the vampires.

When we are a safe distance away, I start walking. My legs ache. Suddenly, a thought dawns on me. *I have super speed and now is the perfect time to try it out!*

"I'll always be watching, Haley," the protector says, reading my facial expression or maybe my feelings.

I can't be sure anymore. "But you must figure some things out for yourself. Now go!"

"Thank you for helping me escape."

The man nods and turns back into a bat. Then he flies away leaving me alone to ponder his statements.

I take a deep breath and concentrate only on running. I picture myself at home with Lana and Alex. The thought of Alex sends a rush of adrenaline all throughout my body and I start to run. Concentrating worked, and I am moving at a blazing speed. I'm home in a few minutes. When I enter my room, Lana is sitting on my bed. I don't take the time to wonder why she's in my room because I am so excited to see her.

"Haley!" she screams as she jumps up and hugs me. I hug her back. "Where were you?" she asks. I tell her my story... from the stranger in my room to me running home.

"Alex and I were so worried!" she tells me.

Alex! "I have to find Alex and tell him I'm alright!" I exclaim.

"Wait, you should know something," she calls.

"It'll have to wait!" I call back. I speed to Alex's house and ring the doorbell. He answers.

"Oh my gosh! Haley! I was so worried about you!" he says hugging me. I feel like I'm on air!

"Let's go out to dinner to celebrate my safe return!" I tell him. *Perhaps this will be our first date!*

"Haley, I'd love to, I really would, but my girlfriend might get mad," he says.

My heart drops to my shoes.

"You and Mandy got back together?" I ask, trying very hard not to let him notice my watering eyes.

He looks confused. "She didn't tell you?"

"Who didn't tell me what?"

"Lana and I are dating."

Chapter 10 - Heartbreak

"What?" I say incredulously.

"Yeah, I thought she told you," he says. That must have been what Lana was trying to say to me before I left. I leave his porch without saying a word. Alex shouts to me but I keep walking, knowing that I cannot hold back the tears anymore.

When I know I'm far enough away, the tears come and don't stop. My stomach aches and my eyes hurt. I go into the nearby woods and lean against a tree. *I can't believe Lana did that to me! She knew I liked him more than anything. She knew that after the break-up, I was going to try to date Alex, or at least get to know him better until he wanted to date again. I get kidnapped, face extreme fear and pain, and what do I come back to? My best friend dating the boy I have wanted to date for so long!*

When I stop crying, I am overcome with an anger that I didn't know I could feel. I speed to my room and Lana is still there. She can tell I've been crying.

"Haley, just hear me out!" she protests.

"How could you do that to me?!" I explode. "You know I like Alex! I went through all that crap and this is what I come back to?!"

"Now, Haley, just listen. I came here to ask you how you were holding up and maybe offer a couple suggestions on how to drop hints to Alex that you liked him, but you were gone. I saw signs of a struggle and went to tell Alex. He waited with me until we figured out a plan of action. I didn't want to call the police because I didn't want to risk them finding out about you. I managed to convince Alex that it was the right thing to do. We started talking and we were both so worried, and then we looked into each other's eyes and we realized how much time we have spent together and then we leaned toward each other, and…and…"

"You kissed him?" I explode, outraged. I storm out of my room and run out to the woods again. More tears start flooding down my cheeks from my already stinging eyes. I climb one of the trees and stay perched up there.

"Haley!" I hear Lana's voice. "Haley, please! I'm sorry this happened! But you have to understand, I really like Alex. Maybe even more than you do! Please, Haley! I'm the only one who can help you! Who else are you going to tell all of this stuff to? Haley!"

I speed higher up in the tree so Lana can't see me. *I don't even know if she is really sorry. She humiliated me and hurt me so bad, that I don't know if I can ever forgive her.* Lana leaves in tears but I feel no sympathy. I climb down and run back to my house. My father is home. *Wait! He knows all about me!*

"Dad, remember when you told me I was going to change in my junior year? But I didn't listen?" I ask him.

He nods. "It's happening now, isn't it?"

"Yeah, but how did you know this would happen to me?"

"Your mother's ancestral line came from a family of vampires. Her father told her that the last vampire in her family was killed years ago. Somewhere along the line, however, one person would become a vampire. They deducted that it would be her child. I knew it was only a matter of time before you started to change. I tried to tell you, but having a boyfriend changed you a lot."

"Dad, it's not fair that I'm the one who has to deal with all this vampire stuff!"

"I know. Don't worry. I'm going to help you through this."

I smile. "Thanks, Dad." I tell him everything that happened to me, including the fact that I have to kill animals in order to feed myself. He listens to everything patiently. Lana comes in through the back door, unexpectedly. Dad leaves the room to let us talk.

"Haley, will you ever forgive me? I know you like Alex a lot, but we are happy together. I want you to be happy for me," she says.

"You broke my heart and you are going to have to deal with the consequences," I say as calmly as possible. *Right now, I need to just handle this maturely.*

"But, Alex and I like each other. We didn't know it until you went missing. Then we both just saw a connection in each other's eyes and we knew exactly what it meant."

"Put yourself in my shoes. Think about before you started dating Alex. Remember how you had that huge crush on Donny?"

Lana's quiet. I know she's thinking about how much she really did like him.

"Now, how would you feel if I dated him?" I ask.

"I guess pretty lousy. You have a right to feel the way you do."

I nod, then speed away out the front door. In my fury, I kick one of the trees, expecting my foot to start throbbing, but instead, the trees falls down. *Great. Super strength -- another thing I have to deal with.*

I hear water. I see a very small waterfall in the distance and I decide to investigate. There is a stream that flows through these woods and the water is falling off some high rocks that must have eroded over time. I smile and jump into the pool of water below the falls. The shimmering water is at a perfect temperature. For a while, I forget all about the problems in my life. I swim around and under the falls in my clothes, as little fish swim near me, tickling my feet. I lie on my back and float on top of the water. The sun is now angling through the trees, creating beautiful rays of light all around the water. *I can't believe I didn't know this was here before!* When I get out, I shake a little water off and speed home. Thankfully, Lana is not there anymore.

I go up to my room and flop onto my bed. *Oh, Lana.*

Soon, I fall asleep.

I hear a noise and open my eyes. I look at my clock. It's three o'clock in the morning. Lana is sitting at the foot of my bed giving me a slight heart attack before I realize it is her.

"Lana, what the heck are you doing here? How did you get in here?" I ask drowsily.

"I snuck out through my window and took my car. You showed me where your spare key was one time when you had forgotten your house key." She sighs. "We need to talk."

"We can talk later when I'm more awake, and tomorrow, I'm changing the location of our spare," I reply, flopping my pillow over my head.

"No, we need to talk now while you are too sleepy to fight me. Haley, I'm sorry. I'm sorry I hurt you. I'm sorry you came back to such bad news. Please forgive me."

"How can I forgive you? You broke my heart. You can't possibly expect me to be happy for you after what you did. We already talked about this." I sit up and look her in the eye. "Get out."

Lana leaves my room reluctantly and I go back to sleep. I hope she never comes into my house again.

Chapter 11 - Clarissa

I have never felt pain deeper than I feel now, and it's all Lana's fault. I pick up my cell. Lana has left me five texts and two voicemails. I delete them all without even reading or listening to them. *She can apologize all she wants, but I will never forgive her for hurting me so much.*

"Haley," a woman's voice whispers. I look around but there is no one there.

"Who are you?" I ask the air.

"I am like you. I left the note on your door."

"The last time someone said that, they ended up kidnapping me."

"Those men worked for me. I am the real sender. They took credit for making it. I asked them to politely go and ask you if you wanted to join me and try to convince you that life would be better with me, but they took things to the extreme. That group of vampires is my special team sent to kill attackers who threaten to expose or destroy us. Basically, they keep us safe. But sometimes the vampires who are assigned this job don't always understand when to be vigorous and when to be gentle and understanding. Therefore, I have had to replace the whole team. But there's no need to worry about the ones who took you. They are...not here anymore."

"So, you're not going to abduct me?"

"Cooperate, and it won't be necessary."

"What do you want me to do?"

"Leave behind this life and join me."

"But everything I love is here!"

"No. Your best friend is dating your crush and your parents are almost never here for you."

I sigh. The voice is right, although I don't know exactly how it knows that. "Where do I go?" I ask.

"Stay in your room. Some of my men will escort you to my headquarters. You do not need to bring anything with you."

"When you say escort…"

"No. No kidnapping or any form of abduction will take place. You would never want to join me then." I say nothing.

I wait about fifteen minutes. There is a knock on my door and I open it. Two men in their early twenties are standing there.

"Come with us, Haley," one of them says.

"Wait," I say. "Let me write a quick note." I grab a post-it note and scrawl out something for Lana, Alex, Mom, and Dad.

Dear Mom, Dad, Lana, and Alex,

   I am leaving. I have found

someone like me. She will take care of me.

Lana, this time I will not come back.

Alex, I want you to know that I've loved

you for a while, but now I know that you

will never be mine.

      Good-bye all. (Forever)

            Haley

   I stick it on my door, take one last glance at my room, and then leave with the men from the only place I've known all my life…my home. We get into a car and drive away. They cover my windows and raise a screen between me and the front seats. I guess they don't want me to see the route that we are taking. We are on the road for at least an hour before we stop and get out. My surroundings are unfamiliar. They are standing in a clearing surrounded by a vast forest. In the center of the clearing is a large one-story building without any windows.

   "Come and meet the woman who was talking to you," one man tells me. I follow them into the strange building. We enter a huge room with row of desks and a wall of computer monitors. I recognize what is on one of the monitors. It is displaying my room.

"Clarissa, we have brought you the girl," one man tells the woman looking at the monitors. She turns and notices me.

"Haley," she says as she stands up and walks over. "I've been expecting you. My name is Clarissa. I am just like you. I am a vampire. I drink blood, I have super-speed, and I have super-strength."

Clarissa has curly, red hair that falls down about an inch below her shoulders. It is clipped to the side. I assume she is in her early twenties and she is wearing jeans and a sweater over a blue t-shirt.

"What is your diet? What type of blood do you drink, I mean?" she asks me.

"Well, I cut myself one time and sucked that blood, which is when I found out that's all I could eat without getting sick. After that, I have only been drinking animal's blood," I explain.

"No human blood?" She seems surprised.

"No! I mean, I think human blood is sweeter, but it's not exactly like I can go to a restaurant and ask for a quart of human blood. And I could never kill anyone for it."

"You have so much to learn! We don't drink the blood from innocent people! We drink from the people who betray us or from those whom the world would be better off without!" she says.

"I…guess…that's okay," I stammer, trying to figure out if she is joking or is really serious.

"But we have to train you. I can tell you, it's hard to stop drinking human blood once you start. You're going to want more and more. It's like an addiction and we cannot let you drink blood from the innocent. Also, seeing as you are a new vampire, you haven't been told how to grow your fangs yet. We will work on that immediately."

She goes to a nearby table with different colored powders and liquids. "I have this here specifically for cases like yours." She pours one powder and liquid after another into a very small bowl and hands the mixture to me. "Drink this, but don't swallow it. Allow the liquid to engulf your upper teeth for a full thirty seconds and then you can swallow."

I take the bowl and tip the concoction into my mouth. It tastes absolutely terrible but I slosh it around before Clarissa gives me a sign to swallow it.

"Now," she says. "You'll feel a bit of pain, but the fangs will begin to grow within seconds."

Suddenly, an extremely sharp pain fills my mouth. I feel two of my upper teeth getting longer and sharper as they protrude down.

"Perfect!" Clarissa exclaims. "Now your fangs will appear only when you want them to. The more you use them, the quicker they will appear. You'll be amazed at how much easier it is to kill things! Now that that part is over with, let's work on controlling your thirst for human blood."

She leads me to another room.

"Just inside this door, we have a few people who abducted some children without my permission; similar to the way you were abducted. Go for the abductor on the right and drink his blood. He will try and resist you, but he should be the easiest to defeat," she explains. She opens the door to the room and we walk in together. Six men are imprisoned in glass tubes. The tubes are large and quite spacey, but I can't imagine being held inside one without going crazy.

"Now, as the abductor's glass case disappears, run and bite his neck as fast as you can," Clarissa says to me. The tube is retracted from one man and he falls. I speed over to him and bite his neck and start drinking. He screams in great pain. I feel awful but his blood is so very, very sweet and delicious that I cannot stop. Soon, he has been reduced to a mere image of his former self.

I feel as though adrenaline is pulsing through my veins. The pleasure I feel is intoxicating. The feeling starts to subside quickly and I begin to feel anxious. *I must have more!*

"Please, give me more! I need more!" I beg.

"No, this is why we practice. You must learn control," she says. I start banging on the glass of the other cages, desperately wanting more blood. Suddenly, two other men drag me out of the room and the door is slammed shut.

"Please, Clarissa! Give me more! I need to satisfy my hunger!"

"Water please, gentlemen," she says.

"I don't want water! I want blood!"

The two men drench me in water. I feel better and no longer have the lust for blood.

"I told you. Human blood is delicious and it will take some time before you no longer go crazy wanting more."

This is going to take awhile!

Chapter 12 - Training

"Don't worry. Everyone who starts drinking human blood goes through the exact same thing," Clarissa says. "It's just that some people don't have anyone to train them, so they become human blood addicts and uncontrollable killers. But we are not like that. We have learned to control our appetites."

"How long did it take you to be able to maintain control?" I ask.

"Well, it varies for everyone. It took me a few weeks, but you seem like someone who could gain control in no time." *She says that like she is positive there is something about me that I don't know.*

I start to feel drowsy and I yawn. It must be very late, but I can't tell for sure because there are no windows here.

"Oh, goodness! You must be exhausted! It's been a long day for you, hasn't it? Let's get you into your room. While my team and I have been observing you, we made an exact replica of your room so that you would be more comfortable when you came to us," she explains.

We walk to another room and she opens the door. *It truly does look exactly like my room, right down to the hole I kicked in the wall when I was little. Even all of my clothes are here as well. That must be why Clarissa told me I don't need to bring anything.*

"No cameras are in here and you are not observed in any way. We trust all our apprentices."

She closes the door and I search the room for cameras to make sure. I find nothing. I focus on my fangs and feel them retract. It stings and takes longer than I expected. Clarissa did say the more I use them, the faster they'll come. I guess it will just take some time. I rub my fingers over my teeth and smile at my accomplishment. I then change into my pajamas, climb into bed, and I fall asleep in seconds.

When I wake up, Clarissa is in my room getting some clothes out of the drawers.

"It's time for practice," she says.

"What?" I say groggily. "Wake me later."

"No time. Get up. Come on. You are never going to fight with us if you don't learn how to control your thirst for blood."

I do want to travel with her. Mostly because she is the only person I trust. When she leaves, I get dressed, and come out of my room. Clarissa is waiting by the door to the room with the glass tubes.

"My team and I needed some food last night, so we have some new additions. There are some girls in there now. They betrayed us and revealed our secret headquarters. They are also new vampires and I never even gave them their fangs yet, so they'll be pretty easy to kill. The person they told is also in there. We can't let her live if she knows about us. Kill her first," she says.

"But I don't want to kill an innocent person," I say.

"She's not exactly all that innocent. We cannot let the world find out about us. She must not live to tell the story."

I make my fangs appear before I walk into the room and stare into the petrified faces of three new people. One of the glass tubes disappears and a girl falls to the ground. She looks up at me and I can see a fear on her face that I have never seen before. I close my eyes so I don't have to look at her when I kill her. I run to her and drink her blood while I try to ignore her screams. When I am done, I don't want anymore, nor do I ever want to drink from a human ever again. That was just too painful. I walk slowly out of the room feeling slightly sick.

"How do you feel this time?" Clarissa asks me.

"Clarissa, that was awful! She looked at me so horribly! And her screams..."

"Well, no one said this was going to be easy. You have to learn to not have any compassion for the people you are killing. It'll get easier as time goes on. I have to say, I'm very impressed that you have gained control of your thirst after only being with us for about a day."

I feel so confused. I thought Clarissa was so nice. She said they never kill innocent people, yet that's exactly what she wants me to do. I go back to my room, if you can even call it that. I begin to miss my old life. I haven't even been gone that long. *I miss Alex and Mom and Dad. I can't believe I'm even thinking this, but I even miss Lana.* My door opens. It's Clarissa.

"I'm sorry you felt the way you did, but my team and I are rather hungry and we would like to save the people in the cases for later. I'll show you the way we kill attackers. We go on the streets and kill anyone who is hurting someone else. We're kind of like vigilantes. I believe that you can agree that the world is better off without them. They are not-so-innocent people and it will be easier for you to kill them."

I get up and got with her outside. Her team is outside at the edge of the forest.

"Just keep close by, Haley. When I stop, you stop," Clarissa tells me. She speeds away and I effortlessly follow her, unsure of exactly where we are heading. When we finally stop, I recognize where we are. San Francisco, California. My hometown is in Virginia. I feel homesick.

"Now, we travel to cities all over the country. When we witness a person being attacked, we come in and 'save the day.' We grab and hold the attacker until the innocent person can escape the scene. Once we're alone with the attacker, we have a meal!" Clarissa explains.

"I don't feel too good about doing this," I say.

"Don't worry. It gets easier every time you do it."

We walk around until we hear someone screaming. We run to the source of the sound and see a man robbing a woman.

"Watch me." Clarissa runs up to the man at light-speed and restrains him by taking his arms and thrusting them upward in the wrong direction. "Go! Run! I've got him!" she yells to the woman.

The woman gets up and runs away as fast as she possibly can. Clarissa pushes the man onto the ground and bites his neck before he can say anything. He screams, but not for long. Clarissa is really quick when she kills. She must have had a lot of practice because she does it so swiftly. She stands up with her back to me. I see her arm come up and it goes across her lips, wiping the man's blood off of her mouth. She then turns to me.

"And that's how it's done." She smiles. "Now, let's find someone else, and you can try it."

We walk a little further until we see two men in a fight. One is now unconscious and the other is about to shoot him.

"Hurry! Don't let him get away!" Clarissa yells and I speed over, grab the gun, and restrain him the way Clarissa showed me. I have never practiced controlling my super-strength, so he pushes me down. He points the gun at me and starts to pull the trigger. Seeing that I'm having trouble, Clarissa speeds over and restrains him quickly.

"Now, Haley! Bite him!"

I don't want to at first, but then I think about how he almost killed a man and wanted to kill me, too. It fills me with anger and fury. I go to his neck and drink. When I am done, I want more and I'm starting to feel the addiction rise up in me. Then a thought hits me. *This addiction must be how it is for my parents. They must be as addicted to alcohol as I am to blood. Addiction is not good and it has consequences. They get drunk and say things they don't mean or sometimes even hurt themselves, and I...kill.* I'm sorry I ever got mad at them. Finally understanding what it's like for them, the craving dies down. More than anything now, I want to see my parents' faces again. I want to see Lana's and Alex's faces too.

"Very good. We'll practice more in a couple days, but we must go back to headquarters now. We all need to rest and I have other apprentices I need to train," Clarissa says.

I follow her as she runs back headquarters--a place where I no longer want to be. One of Clarissa's men opens the door and I trudge to my cloned room. I sit on the bed and think about my past life and how much I would give anything to have it back.

***

I wake up on my own accord for once. I get dressed and exit my room. Clarissa is waiting for me.

"Listen," she says. "I have something to talk to you about. When you gain full control, and when you've perfected your powers and no longer have compassion for the people you kill, you and I would be able to control everything that happens around us. We will have endless power. And you and I would make a pretty good team."

She pauses and continues. "Well, anyway, we have received a new addition last night. It is someone you know and I think you'll be rather excited to kill this girl."

I don't know about that. I don't like killing girls and if it really is someone I know, it will make it all the more difficult.

"Are you ready for this?" she asks. She sounds excited. *What is there to be excited about? Killing people isn't exactly a favorite hobby of mine.* She pushes open the door. I see three faces I've never seen before and one I immediately recognize--the short brown hair, the green eyes, and the familiar necklace.

"Oh, my gosh!" I exclaim. "Lana!"

Chapter 13 - Not So Good

"Let her go, Clarissa!" I command.

"I know how much she hurt you. I thought you would be happy to kill the girl who started dating the boy who was the object of your affection," she says.

"No matter how much Lana ever hurts me, I will never kill her! You may think that every person who does something wrong to you deserves to die, but that doesn't make killing them right. And that is what makes us two totally different people. You were wrong. We will never make a good team. I can't stay with you anymore!"

An awful angry look comes across Clarissa's face. "Fine. If you won't do it, I will get someone who will! Ethan! Get in here!"

A boy not much older than me walks into the room.

She looks at me coldly. "And to think I wanted to share infinite power with you: a girl who can't even kill a guilty person." She turns to Ethan. "Please dispatch of that worthless thing in the third case," she says pointing at Lana.

Lana starts banging on the glass screaming my name, but I can't hear her. The glass is sound-proof.

Ethan starts moving towards Lana's case as Clarissa waves her hand commanding the glass to disappear. I look at Lana, and realize that I've been acting so stupid. I wanted to break up the best friendship I've ever had just because I had a huge crush on some guy.

I'm so sorry, I want to say to her.

My mind reenters the present and I snap as I remember what's about to happen. I am overcome with fear, fury and anger, fighting to find my words.

"Wait!" I speak hoarsely. Ethan turns.

"Get on with it Ethan!" Clarissa screams.

That's when my all my bottled up anger over everything that has happened these past few days just comes out.

"Oh, shut up, Clarissa!!" I scream. It feels good to say that to her. "And Ethan, don't you dare move unless you want your blood drained!"

I turn to Clarissa. "You know, I thought you were nice at first and that you would help me more than anyone from home! I thought you were going to teach me how to take care of myself! But you have gotten me to kill people, and now, you want to capture and kill my friends. I know now that you are not the person I thought you were! Now let Lana go!"

"You really think I would do that?" she laughs. "We don't let people go. They are the meal and there is no other option. Now, drink her blood or I will."

My anger is about to consume me. I start to feel a power growing inside of me and I feel an urge to scream. So I do. It's no ordinary scream; it's a sonic scream. The sonic wave causes Clarissa and Ethan to fall backwards. The glass cases shatter and the people that were inside fall to the ground. Because of the shattered glass on the ground, the fallen prisoners get bloody cuts and scrapes, creating that tantalizing aroma for vampires. Some glass has even gotten wedged into one little boy's leg. A huge desire for the human blood overwhelms me, and it takes all of my strength to save them, not kill them. I pick up the little boy gently and we all begin run out of the room. Ethan gets up and follows us.

"Stop right there! No one move or you are all becoming breakfast!" he shouts.

I step forward a little. "Ethan, I don't want to hurt you, but I will," I say.

He stands frozen to the spot, a cold look on his face, but I can see fear in his eyes. He's not the tough guy he's trying to be. "I mean it! Don't move anymore!"

I try to channel my strength as I did with my speed. I picture myself hitting Ethan. I think about everything Clarissa has done up to now, and I feel my power of strength fill my body. Then I hit Ethan…hard. He flies back and hits the wall. I walk over to him.

"Ethan, come with us. I'll help you. I can undo what Clarissa has done to you. Please, Ethan. I don't want you to kill any more people and I can tell from your hesitation just now that you don't want to kill anymore either."

He gets up and sighs very deeply. He nods, signaling he agrees with me, and follows us. We run to the exit, with me still carrying the little boy, but are abruptly stopped by Clarissa standing in front of it.

"Not so fast! You all have seen too much! You cannot live to tell others!" she growls. She runs to one of the girl's standing behind me and attempts to bite her neck.

"No!" I scream. I hold the little boy with one arm and use the other arm to punch Clarissa before she can take the girl's blood. I punch her as hard as I can and she flies backward and slams into the wall monitors, breaking many of them. I hand the boy to Ethan and speed over to Clarissa. I then make my fangs appear, bite her neck, and I start to drink. She screams and screams, but I keep drinking, actually quite enjoying hearing her cry of agony. She will not kill anyone anymore. Clarissa slumps to the ground. I wipe my mouth and turn towards the others. They are just staring at me and Clarissa's mangled body.

"Let's go! Now! We don't have any time to waste!" I say, taking the little boy from Ethan's arms. We walk out of the strange building, free from everything. I set the boy down on the ground as gently as I possibly can.

"Hey, there, honey. What's your name?" I ask him softly.

"Logan," he answers tearfully.

"Ok, Logan. I'm going to get this piece of glass out, ok? I'm not going to lie to you, it's going to hurt, but I'll get you some medical care as soon as I can."

He nods. I look at the piece of glass digging into his leg. It's bigger than I thought. I sigh and take hold of it. Logan winces. I start to pull slowly. Logan starts screaming and I feel horrible, but I know that it will be worse if I don't get this glass out. All of the other people with us are squeezing his hands and telling him it's okay, comforting him as best they can.

"It's out!" I exclaim. "But we really need to get you to a doctor. Does anyone know the way back?"

"No," another boy answers. "We were all knocked out before we came here."

I sigh again. "Ok, if I speed-run, I can probably figure out where to go to get you all back home. I can only take one of you at a time though and I need to take Logan first, so I can get him to the hospital. Then I'll come back for you guys. I promise. But please, you can't tell anyone about what I can do."

"We would never do that. You're the one who helped us get out of there and prevented us from getting killed. We owe you that," one girl says. The rest of the group agrees.

I smile. "Thanks guys."

I pick Logan up gently and speed-run him to the emergency room. I stay with him while the doctors dress his wound. He calls his parents, and I say good-bye to him. He thanks me for helping me and kisses me on the cheek. He's so adorable. I'm actually pretty upset I probably won't ever see him again. I run back to the Clarissa's headquarters and within six trips, everyone is back in town. They all thank me and start walking home. Lana and Ethan walk with me back to my house.

"Um, Lana, just wait here outside. I'm going to go get Ethan settled," I say.

Ethan follows me inside. I run into my living room. My father is sitting on the couch, watching T.V. I clear my throat. He turns around. The sheer joy on his face when he sees me makes me feel horrible that I ever left. He doesn't say anything. We just hug for a very long time.

"Where were you? Why did you leave us?" he asks.

"It all started with a voice in my room." I continue to tell him about Clarissa and how she was so good to me with at first. Then I told him how I discovered that she was just deceiving me and that she was really evil. I told him how I also managed to pick up a sonic scream. "That's how we all escaped," I explain. "Where's mom?"

My father takes me to the couch. Whatever happened can't be good.

"When we showed your mother the note you wrote, she took it very hard. She was drunk and not herself. Her emotions weren't the same." He sighs. "Honey, you're mom…she left us. She didn't even take anything with her. She just got into her car and drove off."

The air turns to ice. I can't move. I can't breathe. I can't even cry. I just get up and take Ethan to the guest room.

"Ethan, just stay here," I say shakily. I go back downstairs and out to my front yard. Lana is still sitting down on the grass. She notices my pale and rigid face and runs up to me. She knows that I heard the news about Mom's departure. I can tell she wants to hug me, but I know she's not sure if I have forgiven her. So I hug her. I cry and cry as she hugs me back tightly.

"I'm sorry, Lana," I choke out through my tears.

"Oh, it's okay. Listen to me. I was the first one to find your note and I realized I am absolutely the worst best friend in the world to do that to you. Even if Alex and I do like each other, it is not worth it to see you so miserable and mad like you were. I didn't even like him as much as I said I did. Maybe I was just that desperate for a boyfriend. I talked to Alex and I told him about your feelings and how you were better for him. And, uh, we broke up," she tells me.

"What? I'm sorry about how I acted. I let my jealousy get the best of me. You didn't have to do that."

"Haley, you and Alex are better for each other. Anyone can see that. I'm truly sorry for hurting you like I did. I won't ever do that to you again."

"You are the best friend I have ever had in my life, and I don't want to ruin it just because I'm jealous." I pause, thinking about what is really happening right now. "I just found about Mom." I start crying again and Lana hugs me. "She really is gone, isn't she?" I ask. I don't want a response. I feel like I'm in this awful nightmare, from which I'll never wake up. My eyes are red and burning. I never knew I could feel this kind of pain.

"Do you want me to stay with you?" Lana asks.

"No, I want some time alone," I answer.

"Ok, I'll see you tomorrow."

I nod and walk up to the bathroom. I pass the guest room and see Ethan is sitting on the bed. I clean my face up and fix my hair, then go back to the guest room and show Ethan around my house. "The only way I can keep track of you and make sure you stay out of trouble is to keep you here. I hope you'll be happy. Now, if you are hungry, please tell me. You are not going to drink human blood anymore. The only blood you will drink will be from animals. Killing people is wrong, no matter what Clarissa told you. So do not leave this house without me," I explain. "Now just stay here and get some rest."

I leave the room and close the door behind me. Then, I trudge to my room. I change, get into bed, and I cry myself to sleep.

Chapter 14 - Ethan

My throat is raw when I wake up. I must have been from screaming. I dreamt about Mom. It is all my fault that she left us. I look in my bathroom mirror and notice my cheeks are still very red and puffy. I change, brush my hair, and go downstairs. Ethan is in the kitchen with my dad.

"Good morning! I knew you brought someone home yesterday, but after all of the trauma and hearing about Mom, I knew you were too upset to tell me much about him. Ethan is a nice young man. I'm glad I have had the pleasure of meeting him," he says while cooking up some eggs and bacon. Ethan is helping him.

I smile. "Ethan and I are going to go to the woods now and go have some breakfast and training time."

"Alright, but be careful." he says.

Ethan and I hop into my car because just once I want to do things the normal way instead of the vampire way.

"How are you holding up?" he asks, trying to make conversation. I shrug and observe him as best as I can out of the corner of my eye. He is shy and has short dirty-blonde hair. He's a little taller than I am.

"It's going to take awhile," I say.

After a few moments of silence, he asks, "Do you really think you can change me from drinking human blood to drinking animal blood?" he asks me.

"I'm sure I can."

We arrive at the woods and I go to the location of my traps. *Now that I have learned to channel my super strength and speed, I probably don't need these anymore. But I guess I'll still keep them for days when I don't have time to hunt.*

"Wait!" Ethan says so suddenly, I almost trip trying to stop. "I've never had anything other than human blood. What if I can't do it? I mean, I saw you when you had your first human blood. What if it's like that for me?"

"Ethan, you can do it. You just need to find the will to do it," I urge.

He sighs deeply. I make my fangs appear and suck the blood out of the rabbit in my trap. Clarissa was right about one thing: it is so much easier to suck the blood out of animals this way!

I see a raccoon scamper a few feet from us and figure that now is a better time than any other to try to catch animals with my powers. Raccoons aren't that fast, so with super speed I easily chase it down and grab it by the fur on its back. The raccoon starts to squirm and tries to scratch me with its claws. But I grab the raccoon's head with my other hand and then sink my head into its neck. It stops struggling as I quickly drain its blood. I turn to Ethan. "You do have super strength and speed, right?"

He nods.

"Alright, now you need to do what I just did. The animal might scratch you, but in the end you get a meal!"

We hunt quietly for a little while until I spot a fox.

"Remember what I did," I whisper.

Ethan runs up to the fox and quickly bites its neck. The fox squeals, but I see him keep drinking. He tosses the fox's drained body aside and runs back to me.

"It's not as sweet as human blood!" he screams in my face.

"I know, but we cannot be killers anymore. You have to drink animal's blood. I know it's not as sweet, but you'll just have to become accustomed to the taste."

"I need human blood!" he says frantically. "I can only drink human blood! That's how Clarissa trained me! You were wrong! You can't change me!"

I get an idea. "Alright, fine. Follow me back to my house. I've got a human there you can have."

He follows me back to my car and I drive us back home.

"Where's the human?" he asks as we step inside.

"In my kitchen," I say slyly. I grab the spray nozzle off of my kitchen sink and spray Ethan with it. If there's anything I learned from my mistake of going with

Clarissa, it's that water makes a lust for blood, human or animal, go away immediately.

"I'm so sorry! I didn't mean to yell at you!" he says after his head clears.

"Ethan, believe me. I know what it's like. When Clarissa was training me I needed more and more blood the first time. Hearing the people's agony was just too much for me, though, and it became really hard for me to drink their blood."

I go up to my room, flop on my bed, and just lay there staring at the ceiling. Then I remember I haven't seen Alex since I left. I run out of my room.

"Ethan, I'll be right back! I have to go see someone! Don't go anywhere until I come back!" I shout to him as I run out the door. I speed-run down to Alex's house and knock on the door. He answers again, but he doesn't hug me like he did before.

"Hi, Haley," he says quietly. "Glad to see you're back."

"Is something wrong?" I ask.

"Well, Lana probably told you that we broke up."

I nod.

"I saw your note and, uh, I just need to tell you something."

My heart starts racing. *Is he going to tell me he loves me?*

"Haley, you need to get over me. We just aren't meant to be together."

At that point my heart rips in two. I feel like I've just been punched in the stomach. My eyes start to get blurry, but I try to hide it.

"Um, yeah, I totally get it," I say, my voice cracking. "Bye," is all I can say. I start to walk away.

"Haley, wait. Hold on," he shouts to me.

"I don't care, okay Alex? Let's just move on and forget about it!" I scream at him. I slowly run into the woods and tears start to flow down my cheeks. My eyes sting and I'm getting a splitting headache. I speed-run to Lana's house. She's lying on her stomach on the grass in her front lawn, wearing a pretty spring shirt and jeans while reading a book. She sits up and notices me.

"Oh my gosh! What happened?" she asks, quickly getting up.

"It was Alex!" I sob. "He said to get over him because we're never going to date. But I can't! You can't just get over someone you have had a crush on for a year!"

"It'll be really hard, I know, but I think if you give it time, you'll find yourself able to get over him. Do you want me to go talk to him?"

"No. Will you stay the night please?"

"Ok, come on," she says.

We walk back to my house. When we walk in the door, Ethan comes running.

"Hey, what's wrong?" he asks quietly, seeing my facial expression.

Lana shakes her head and Ethan turns and walks away. We go up to my room and Lana locks the door behind us. A few minutes later there's a knock. It's Dad.

"Haley, are you ok?" he asks through the door.

Lana goes and opens the door. She steps out and I assume she's explaining what happened with Alex to my dad. Then she steps back in.

"Your dad says he's sorry and he hopes you feel better. I said it was best not to talk to you at the moment," she explains. She sits down on my bed next to me. "I'm sorry."

I'm a mess from crying this much. "Alex hates me," I say, even though I know it's not true.

"No, he doesn't. He just wants to be friends."

"No, he hates me. He never wants to talk to me again."

"Haley, come on now. You know he doesn't hate you. I'm going to go talk to him about it tomorrow, ok? Maybe I can find out why he said that to you. I honestly think he likes you, so I don't understand why he said something like that."

I sniff and wipe my eyes.

No one bothers me for the rest of the day because Ethan and Dad know to stay away. Lana and I stay up until two in the morning just talking about everything that has happened.

***

I dream about Mom and Alex. Alex's words keep ringing in my head. I toss and turn for most of the night.

When daytime comes, Lana gets dressed and eats breakfast at my house, while Ethan and I take a quick trip to the forest for our breakfast. He seems be adjusting to the taste, but I still have to dowse him with water when he becomes crazed with hunger for human blood.

As soon as Lana finishes eating, she says goodbye, and walks back to her house.

I pass Ethan in the living room, he asks me, "Are you okay now?"

"Yeah, just, my eyes kinda hurt," I say.

"Haley, um, I—" Ethan gets cut off by my cell phone buzzing in my pocket.

Lana had sent me a text. *"**hey, I just left alex's house. on my way over. ive got a lot to tell u.**"* I get anxious when I read the text.

When Lana arrives a couple minutes later, I say to Ethan, "Uh, Ethan, you can just keep hanging out here. Lana and I need to talk about some personal stuff."

"Come on," Lana says to me.

I can already feel my heart re-breaking.

Chapter 15 - The News

"So, the first thing I asked him was what did he do to you," Lana starts. "He repeated what you told me he had said to you. Well, I got a little irritated because it was worse coming from his mouth, so I yelled at him."

"What did you say?" I ask.

"I said, 'How could you do that?! Haley's been crying her eyes out because of you!' And, well, he looked like he felt pretty bad. He said he didn't mean to hurt you, but I told him he did and that he couldn't undo it. He said to tell you he was sorry and he wants to talk to you about it. He said he felt awful and wanted to make it up to you. I told him he obviously liked you and that he was just denying it. I kept on badgering him, and he finally exploded at me. He yelled at me to go and leave him alone. So I did."

Her cell phone buzzes as a new text messages comes into display.

"Alex sent me a…rather long text message," she says.

"What did he say?" I ask.

"He said he's sorry for yelling at me, and again, he feels really bad about hurting you. He also said that he didn't mean to lead you on. He was just trying to be friends and then see where that led him."

Lana hugs me tightly.

"I'm so sorry things aren't working out for you. The truth is, you're too good for him. Alex doesn't know what he's missing. You're so smart, and pretty, and nice, and if he's too dumb to see that, then you don't need him anyway."

I smile, just a little bit.

"I'll stay with you again tonight, ok?" says Lana.

I nod. "Text Alex back and say I'm over him now. And I hope he's happy," I say stubbornly.

Lana nods and whips out her cell phone. She has always been able to text at lightning speed. Seconds later, Alex texts back.

"He said he feels awful and he's far from happy, and…" Lana falters.

"What? What else did he say?"

"He said he sort of liked you, but he got scared about it. He doesn't even know why. "

"Really?" I ask, smiling ever so slightly. Alex never did make sense that way.

"Yeah. Listen, Alex was just worried about you and paranoid about liking you. Maybe because he and Mandy broke up and then I dumped him and he's just not ready to date yet."

I get up off the bed and walk towards the window. My mind is racing with all of this twisted information.

"You know, I think I'll fine by myself tonight. I just need some time to think," I say.

"Ok, but call me if you need anything," Lana says, walking to the door. Just as she's about to leave, she turns to me and adds, "I really think you should talk about this with him." Then she's gone.

I lay against my headboard, hugging my knees to my chest. I'm aching all over, but my heart is very slowly patching back together.

***

Several weeks pass as I continue to train Ethan to drink only animal's blood and cope with what Alex said to me and my own vampire changes.

Ethan and I spend hours together every day, getting to know each other more and more. His lust for human blood finally begins to diminish and our hunts become something we both look forward to each day. We quickly become inseparable, living in sync with one another. The weeks become a month and more, and I find that the hurt from Alex is fading.

One day, as I'm up in my room retrieving something for Lana while she waits downstairs, I hear something that makes me shudder.

"Haley," an eerie voice whispers.

My eyes get very wide. *The last time I heard this voice in my room, it was Clarissa telling me to go and live with her.*

"Haley, I'm back," it whispers again.

"Who are you?" My voice trembles from the fear that it might actually be *her*. I killed her….didn't I?

"You know this voice. Vampires don't die if someone drinks their blood, as long as there is someone there to care for them and heal them."

"Clarissa?" I squeak.

"Yes, I'm back, Haley. From the moment I met in you in person, I knew you were different. You're not like other vampires. I still need your skills to complete the tasks I have in my mind. And this time, the choice is not yours!"

At that moment, the window behind me flings open and two strong arms grab me from behind. One hand goes over my mouth and the other goes around my arms. But this person made the mistake of not having chloroform to subdue me. I am awake and stronger than ever. I have been honing my skills for over a month since we last met. I bite the hand and the person shouts. By the sound of the shout, I can tell it's a man.

"Lana!" I scream as loud as I possibly can. The hand goes back over my mouth and tries to pull me to the window.

"Haley?" I hear Lana's voice. Then I hear pounding footsteps. I stomp on the man's right foot. He howls in pain and removes his hand again. He pulls out a knife and puts it near my throat, daring me to move. Lana comes barging in, but freezes as soon as she sees what is going on in my room.

"Help me," I whisper.

"What are you doing?" Lana asks softly.

"Orders. I gotta take her back," says the man.

"Ok, but just wait. I have someone you could take instead, and he'll go willingly."

She runs back out my door. My mind is racing… trying to figure out what she is up to. She comes back in and Ethan is with her.

"Ethan?" the man rasps.

"Now, Ethan!" Lana screams to him.

Ethan runs at lightning speed and knocks the knife out of the man's hands. I'm released from his iron grip. Everything that I have practiced for the past month comes into play now. My fangs now appear the second I think about them. Ethan is struggling so I jump on the man from behind and try to bite his neck. He scrunches his shoulders so that I can't reach his neck. So I jump off his back and reach for his knife on the floor at lightning speed. Then with super strength, I plunge the knife into his back. He's weakened and I can finally bite his neck. Ethan drinks the blood spurting out of the knife wound. No one's going to be there to heal this man. To make sure of it, Ethan and I drag his body to the nearby woods and bury him.

Finally it is done and we speed-run back to my room.

"Who was that?" Lana asks. "And how did he know Ethan?"

Ethan and I look at each other.

"He was her henchman," I say, as if in a trance.

"Who's henchman?"

"Clarissa. She's back."

Chapter 16 - Love

There is silence in the room for a long time.   I know Lana's probably thinking about her last run-in with that terrible woman.

"I thought you killed her," she finally says softly.

"She said vampires don't die if there's someone there to heal them in time. I guess her henchmen healed her," I say.

"Yeah, it's true.   I've seen Clarissa heal her henchmen before," Ethan says. After a few moments, he says, "Haley, I really need to tell you something."

"What is it?"

"Um, I…" he starts. He then whispers something so quietly, I can't hear him at all.

"What did you say?"

"   "

"Ethan, you're going to have to speak up."

"I --"

"Ethan, behind you!" Lana suddenly screams.

Another henchman bursts through the door and bites Ethan's neck, obviously thinking he was me. *Why is Clarissa trying so hard to capture me?*

All of a sudden, the bat—my protector—flies in through my window and turns into his human self. He swiftly delivers a blow to the henchman which knocks him out. My protector then drains the man of all blood.

"I told you I'd always be watching and I would protect you whenever I could. I was about to help you before, but you, Lana, and Ethan had everything under control. You need to help Ethan now." Then he morphs into a bat again carrying the man in his teeth, which is an amazing sight in itself.

I run back over to Ethan. I sit down beside him and cradle his head in my arms. I press my hand against his neck to try to slow the blood loss.

"Come on, Ethan," I say soothingly. My eyes start to water. "You can't leave me now."

"Haley," he gasps.

"Ssshhh, don't talk."

"Haley, I love you."

There is silence. My ears start to ring in the utter quiet.

"I've been trying to tell you."

A tear rolls down my cheek. "I love you too."

After everything I went through with Alex, I now realize that I've been blind to my feelings for Ethan. He was always concerned about me, and never hurt me, like Alex did. I knew deep down that I had felt something stirring inside me, feelings for him I couldn't explain.

I look at Lana. "He's losing so much blood." Then, I look at Ethan. "Did Clarissa ever tell you exactly how to heal a vampire?" I ask through my tears.

Ethan gasps harshly.

"I saw her do it once." He pauses. "Blood. I need to be fed human blood," he whispers.

"Let me go get some scissors. I'll cut myself."

"No, it must be blood from a non-vampire."

We both look at Lana. She kneels down beside him.

"I'll do it for you, Ethan," she says. She grabs my very sharp scissors off of my desk and slices her hand. She winces and I have to look away. Seeing Lana do that to herself is just too much for me to see.

"Hurry! I've only got seconds left," Ethan chokes out.

Lana squeezes her hand tightly, and lets a solid stream of blood drip out and into Ethan's mouth. His eyes close and his body goes limp.

"Ethan?" I ask frantically.

I start to cry softly until I notice that the bite mark on Ethan's neck is slowly disappearing. All of a sudden, Ethan inhales deeply and sits upright. We all join in a big, long group hug.

Suddenly, Ethan kisses me—right on the lips! At first, I'm surprised, but then I find myself kissing back.

I few minutes later hear the doorbell ring, which shakes Ethan and I out of our little "moment." Ethan is sitting up and looking much better now, so I run out of my room and answer the door.

Alex is standing there. *What in the world is he doing here? How does he have the nerve to break my heart, not talk to me for almost two months, and then show up at my front door?*

"Haley –" he starts.

"What do you want Alex?" I snap, cutting him off.

"Uh, Lana told me what happened, um, after I spoke to you last," he explains. "I've wanted to explain myself to you, but I could never find a good time to do so. Listen, I feel terrible about hurting you. I wasn't trying to be mean, but I thought you needed to know. I mean, I guess I did come on a little too strong. But it wasn't my in–"

"Haley!" Ethan calls. I hear him coming down the stairs.

"Hey," I say. He pulls me into a hug and a kiss. "Oh, um, Ethan, this is Alex," I say after he pulls away.

"Oh, the 'Mr. Broke-The-Heart-Of-My-Girl' guy," he says.

I'm a little surprised Ethan actually said that to Alex because he's always seemed so shy and it looked like he didn't even have the capability to be rude to someone unless he was in a craze for blood. I guess being in love with me has made him a little possessive. But I say quickly to avoid a possible fight, "Ethan, it's okay. I'm happy that I'm with you now."

Alex's face has turned very pale by now, which doesn't make sense. He hasn't called me in almost two months, and he was the one who told me he wasn't into me. He just turns around and walks away.

"You didn't have to kiss me in front of him," I say.

"I wanted him to feel the hurt you felt," Ethan replies.

He kisses me and then turns away and heads back upstairs. I stand there motionless for a while as I think about what he said. He's right, Alex deserved that.

Just as I am about to close the door, yet another henchman dressed in black comes in through the door and I feel a sharp pain on the back of my head before I lose consciousness.

***

I wake up, and my head is pounding. I slowly sit up and see Clarissa standing above me.

"I've got to hand it to you and your pals," she chuckles. "You are very tough, resistant, and resourceful. It took me three tries to finally capture you and I lost two of my best men. I can't believe you managed to heal Ethan. I thought for sure that no one in your little posse knew how to heal vampires."

Her ugly smile fills me with rage.

"I will never do anything for you," I say weakly. "I would rather die."

"That can be arranged," she growls. "Unfortunately, I cannot take pleasure in such an act because I need you and your powers." She comes up to me, her face centimeters away from mine, and exhales slowly. A strange, blue mist comes out of her mouth and quickly enters mine. I feel a strange sensation flood my body – undoubtedly the mist taking affect. As the mist makes its way to my brain, I become dizzy for a moment. Then a sensation overcomes me. I suddenly feel the need to obey Clarissa. After all, she took me in when all hope was lost for me. Sure she wanted me to kill, but I understand why now, and she had a good reason for wanting me to do so.

I smile. "What do I do first?" I ask.

Clarissa laughs. "I've got many things for you to do. First, I want you to kill your little friend, Ethan."

Even with this new need to obey her, I struggle when I hear this first command. "Why should I kill him? What wrong has he done?" I must understand why I'm killing the boy who loves me. Even though I love him, the urge to do what Clarissa wants is stronger.

"He betrayed us by not obeying me and aiding you and my prisoners to escape from me. He must be punished for abandoning me."

I gasp. Emotions are starting to evaporate. *How could anyone leave Clarissa? I'm now mad at myself for previously leaving such a wonderful woman.*

"I also know that he has feelings for you and you have feelings for him. I don't want that to blind you from seeing how much you need me," she adds.

"Your wish is my command. How shall I get rid of him?"

"Try to make it as painful as possible. He deserves it."

"I know how to do it. Would you like anything else?"

"Just get that job done first. Then please come back here for more orders. I expect this to be a quick killing. After all, like I said before, there are so many things for you to do."

"Of course," I say, walking away to complete my first task from the greatest person on earth.

Chapter 17 - Something Strange

Clarissa said I had to kill Ethan as painfully as possible. So the first thing I have to do is crush his heart into a thousand pieces. His blood will be so appealing to me. I speed home and call Ethan's name. He comes running and pulls me into another kiss.

"Where have you been the last couple of hours?" he asks. "It's like you just disappeared."

"That's none of your business."

"What's wrong, baby?" he asks.

"Don't call me 'baby!'" I snap. I never knew how good it felt to yell at someone like this! "Look Ethan, you're a great guy and all, but I will never get over Alex! You can kiss me all you want. There will never be a spark!"

He looks at me with extreme disbelief. I try to resist the urge to smile with the great satisfaction I feel.

"And one more thing..." I add, but I don't finish the sentence. There's no need to. I go for his neck and take a nice bite. He screams and Lana and Dad come running into the room. Lana's wrist and hand are wet for some reason.

"Haley, what are you doing?" Lana exclaims.

I stand up, blood dripping from my mouth. "I must kill the betrayer!" I rasp.

She pauses before she realizes what's happened. "Clarissa's done something to you. Haley, what did she do to you? This isn't you!"

"You don't know anything about me!"

"Yes, I do! And I know you well enough to know that this isn't yourself talking, and you would never kill Ethan!

I notice that Lana's hand is still dripping from the cut she made earlier. Why didn't she clean it or dress it at all? That must've been what she was doing when Ethan screamed. At this point, Lana seems to remember her hand is still bleeding. She runs up to Ethan and lets blood drop into his mouth.

I start to move toward Ethan to finish the job before he can be revived. Lana puts up her other hand and yells, "Stop, Haley!" She stares me down, yet I see fear in her eyes. She's scared because she doesn't know who I've become or what I will do next. "You will have to kill me first before you touch Ethan."

Suddenly I feel emotions arise in me again. Clarissa told me to kill Ethan, not Lana. I can't kill Lana – she is my best friend. But Lana said I have to kill her first. My brain starts to hurt and I feel confused. *What do I do?*

I stare back at her before I turn and speed-run back to Clarissa, extremely frustrated that I failed her.

"Is the task done?" she asks.

I don't want her to know that I failed; that Ethan is still living.

"Yes," I lie. "Ethan is no more."

She smiles, and I feel guilty. "Good. Now I have one tiny thing I need you to do for me. I want you to give me your powers."

"But I need those. How else will I complete your other tasks?"

"Calm down! All I want is your super-strength and your sonic scream. You can keep your super speed."

I comply and stand still in front of her, ready for whatever she must do to extract my powers from me.

She inhales deeply with satisfaction. As she inhales, blue mist comes out of my mouth and back into Clarissa's. Just enough of the blue mist leaves my body to allow my mind to come back into focus and register what she has done to me. I reach for Clarissa and attempt to bite her, but she fights back, not wanting a repeat of her last near-death experience. She did not consume my powers, so I try to do everything in my power to defeat and kill her, but she just mirrors my movements. Through my rage at her, I let out a long, powerful scream and she falls to the ground, blood dripping from her ears. I quickly bite her neck and drain her of her blood.

"I'm going to make sure you don't live this time," I say hoisting her up on my shoulders and escaping her headquarters. I speed-run home.

"Lana, help me!" I yell as I arrive at my house. Lana comes running to me. Her hand isn't wet anymore, but she still has a nice gash. At first, she just stares at the body I've brought with me.

"Where's Ethan?" I ask frantically.

"Um, he's upstairs. What do you need?" she asks.

"I need to know how to get rid of Clarissa for good."

"You need to rip her apart and dispose of the body," Lana says matter-of-factly.

"Remind me to ask you how you knew that later," I say running to the forest. Once there, I rip her body to shreds. It makes me gag. I use my super strength to dig a hole and bury Clarissa's body. It's done. I am positive this time that she will never kill again. I speed home once again.

"Lana, where is Ethan?" I demand.

"You need to talk to him. He's in his room," she tells me.

I go to the guest room and knock on the door, but I don't wait for a reply. I just walk right in, knowing Ethan probably wouldn't have let me in anyway. He is sitting on the bed.

"Hey, Ethan. Listen, I know a small apology will never really make up for it, but I'm so sorry I tried to kill you. It was Clarissa. She did something to me and tried to take some of my powers. I'm also really sorry about what I said. You know me. I would have never said that on purpose," I explain.

He stands up. "I know what she did. I've seen her do it before. But the point is, it hurt because I realized that it was true."

I start to say something, but pause. I think about what he said. *He's right. It was true.*

"Ethan –"

"Just go," he whispers.

"Ok, look!" I scream in defense. "Maybe it was true! But you are always there and haven't hurt me like Alex did! I thought you were "the one" for me, but I guess I was wrong!"

"Get out of here!" he bellows.

I start to yell back that it was my house, but decided just to leave anyway. But I leave in anger. Not really at Ethan, but at my luck or lack of it. *It's not fair that something bad always happens between me and the guys I like.* Lana comes up to me. She had heard the whole thing. Before she can say anything, the doorbell chimes.

"I'll answer it," I say without looking at her. I walk over to the door and whip it open. I can't believe my eyes. It's Mandy!

"Hey girl!" she exclaims, hugging me. "I haven't seen you in a while! Where ya been?"

"Um, hi, Mandy," I say a little confused. *What the heck is Mandy doing here? It's not like her to just show up without calling me first.* "Well, I've just been a little busy," I tell her. *She has no idea!*

"Well, I just thought we could hang out if you have time."

At that moment she blinks and I can see the faintest shade of bright red in her eyes. But when she blinks again, it disappears. I shrug it off as Lana comes up behind me, equally shocked that Mandy is here.

"Mandy was just saying that she wants to hang out with me," I say.

"Yeah, I mean, I haven't seen you in a while, so I thought it would be fun for the two of us," Mandy chimes in.

Mandy has always loved group dates, so I am surprised when she says "the two of us." That implies she wants to hang out with me. I look at Lana. I can tell from Lana's face that she is surprised and has registered the hint. "Uh, you know what? You guys go ahead," she interjects. "I actually have a lot of stuff to do at my house. Have fun." Lana gets inside her car and drives off. *That was awkward.*

"What do you want to do?" I ask Mandy.

"I'm in the mood for a horror flick. What about *Jaws of Death*? It's supposed to be the scariest, goriest movie they've ever come out with!"

"Um, ok," I say. The fact that Mandy wants to go see that movie really surprises me. She had never been one to like scary movies. The only reason she went to go see *Ghostly Fears* during that group hang-out was because Alex wanted to go. *What is up with her?*

"Great! Come on! There's a movie showing in 20 minutes!" She grabs my hand and we run to her car.

When we arrive at the theater, we purchase our tickets and Mandy gets some soda and popcorn. She asks me if I want anything, but I tell her I'm not hungry. So we find some really good seats. As soon as the movie is over, I realize that Mandy is right. That was the bloodiest movie I have ever seen. Although it actually made me a bit hungry, it was definitely scary! I screamed on several occasions.

"Well, did you like it?" she asks.

"That was... definitely surprising!" I say hesitantly.

She laughs. "Come on, let's get out of here. There's something I need to tell you in the car."

As we stroll out to the parking lot, I have to resist the temptation to just speed over to our parking place. We get into her car, both of us silent and on edge. When Mandy starts to drive home, she says five words that almost make my heart stop.

"I know you're a vampire."

"What are you talking about?" I try to laugh.

"You always were a terrible liar, Haley. Give it up. I know you only drink blood and that you have several different powers."

"How'd you know?"

"That's for me to know and you to find out," she gloats.

There is silence for a while.

"Don't worry," Mandy finally says. "Now that I know, we don't have to keep driving everywhere. You can just use your super-speed to get us places and we can get there in half the time."

I feel a little hurt at first because I realize that Mandy is using me. But I just say, "What about Lana? We always do everything together."

"Well, sometimes you just need to get away from your old friends and hang out with some new ones or ones you don't hang out with as much. I'm sure she'd understand. After all, I saw her kissing Alex in her car."

I didn't think I could take much more hurt, but there it was. I'm not really mad that they kissed because I'm over Alex now, but I'm more mad at the fact that Lana lied to me. "What?" I say quietly.

"Oh, you didn't know? Well, I guess I just assumed since you two tell each other everything. But yeah, I saw them making out in her car."

"No, Lana wouldn't do that to me."

"Wouldn't she? Come on, she already dated him. I guess they liked each other too much to call it off forever, but they didn't want to hurt you again, so they didn't tell you."

"It doesn't matter. Alex is a thing of the past anyway."

"Please. I know you still have feelings for him."

"Why would you think that?"

"Because it's how I felt after he broke up with me."

Luckily, we pull into my driveway at that moment.

"Thanks for the ride, Mandy," I say, numbly.

"No prob. Sorry that you had to find out from me. But you do deserve to know."

I run inside, go up to my room, lock the door, and sink down against it.

"Haley?" Lana calls, knocking on the door two hours later. I had stayed locked up in my room ever since I got back from the movies.

I can't believe she has the nerve to even try to talk to me! "Go away."

"Haley, what is it?"

"You should know, back-stabber," I say quietly, so that Lana doesn't hear me.

I run to my window, jump out and land perfectly on the ground. Being a vampire really has its advantages. I run to the forest--my special place. At this point I realize I am hungry and swiftly catch a nearby squirrel with ease. I drink some blood from it and just walk around, numb, for a while. I take Mom's picture out of my pocket. I've been carrying it ever since she left.

"Mom, what am I supposed to do? Lana said she would never do anything with Alex because of how much it hurt me. She lied. Please help me. I'm so confused and upset."

I pour out all my feelings to her picture for an hour and a half until I feel better. It may sound strange, but it was almost like she was there with me.

"Thanks Mom. I love you." I kiss my fingertips and place them to her picture. Then I begin to walk home leaving my troubles behind me in the forest.

Chapter 18 - Mandy

I speed-run home, and immediately when I walk in the door, Lana grabs my arm. I suppose she decided to stay here until I got home just so she could corner me and force me to tell her what Mandy said to me.

"Haley, what did I do?" she asks firmly.

"You should know," is all I say stubbornly.

"But I don't. Tell me!"

"Mandy said she saw you and Alex kissing inside your car!"

"What?! We never did that! I haven't even talked to Alex since that day I accused him of hurting you so much!"

"Oh, so now you're going to lie to me about it?!"

"I can't believe you of all people would accuse me of lying to you! We've known each other for years! I would never lie to you!"

"Look, you dated Alex, and then you broke up with him. Who's to say you two wouldn't want to get back together?"

"I told you! I'd be a horrible friend if I did that to you again, and I didn't even like him as much as I said I did. And he's not exactly the guy for me anyway! And what do you even care? I thought you were over him!"

I pause. "Look me in the eye and tell me you didn't kiss Alex in your car."

Lana looks straight at me. Those bright green eyes seem to stare right through me. Not even once straying her eyes she states, "I did not kiss Alex in my car."

I sigh very deeply and look at her sheepishly. "Ok, you've convinced me. But if you're telling the truth, then that means Mandy lied to me. Why would she do that? She's not like that. In fact, she's been doing a lot of things that aren't like her lately."

"Maybe she just thought it was me and Alex," says Lana in a cool tone. Lana's such a good friend to still keep her cool even after I screamed at her.

We don't say anything for awhile, and just stand there awkwardly.

"Sorry for yelling at you," I apologize.

Lana smiles. The only thing we can do is walk away from each other, leaving the silence in the room.

The next afternoon, the doorbell chimes right after I get back from drinking a little blood in the woods. I go to answer it and it's Mandy again!

"You're back?"

"We had so much fun yesterday, that I thought we could do something else today!"

"Can Lana come too?"

"Wait, what? I thought you were still mad about her kissing Alex!"

"No, she said she didn't and I think I believe her." She looks disappointed as if her "plan" didn't work.

"Well, you guys spend too much time together. Why don't you just hang out with me? We never have just the two of us."

I'm actually *really* angry at her for lying about something like that, but the only way to figure out what's up with her is to hang out with her.

"Yeah, I guess you're right. Dad!" I call through the door. "I'm going out! I'll be back whenever!"

Mandy and I walk to a popular restaurant nearby, but only she orders because I tell her I just ate lunch. When Mandy orders her food, we wait over forty-five minutes and it never arrives. Mandy raises her hand above her head and snaps at our waitress who just happened to be nearby.

"Hey!" she calls. "We've been waiting almost an hour for our food!"

"Mandy, it's ok."

"No, it's not ok!" she answers, standing up. She puts her face closely to the waitress's and starts screaming, "The service here is terrible! We shouldn't have to wait this long for a small order! It's not even that busy here! I want to see food in front of me on the table in two minutes, or else I will personally go talk to the manager and report the lazy waitress that was serving us!"

The look on the waitress's face is incredulous. There's shock, anger, and humiliation all at once.

Mandy sits back down. "I think that did the trick," she giggles.

"Mandy, what's up with you?" I ask. "You're not usually like this."

She grins. "It's the new me!"

I liked the old Mandy; the one who was nice to everyone, who was a true friend.

Her food does come about a minute later.

"Told you it worked!" Mandy laughs triumphantly.

I decide not to say anything. When she finishes eating, we both walk into an alley beside the restaurant where no one can see us. She hops on my back and I speed-run us toward home. Mandy squeals in excitement as I speed off.

"We should go shopping tomorrow night! See you at 8!" Mandy says getting into her car before I can even say anything. I stare off in the direction she drove.

After she leaves I begin thinking of my discussion with Lana earlier. *I believe Lana more so than Mandy, so why would Mandy lie? And she totally blew off the fact that I caught her in a lie. Alex is in the center of this love triangle – all three of us have liked him. Wonder if he knows what's going on with Mandy? I should talk with him just as Lana said. No, he'll think I'm crazy. And I don't even know if I'm ready to talk to him yet.* I call it a night and go inside.

The next night, after an extremely busy day, I look at the clock on my wall, and its 7:50 PM. Mandy will be here soon. I decide to drink some animal blood before she gets here. When I walk in the door, Mandy is in the kitchen talking to my dad.

"Hey, girl! Ready to go on a major shopping spree? After all, you do need a wardrobe change!"

I'm a little offended, but we leave and head to the mall in her car. We decide the car is better because bags would be hard to carry if I were speed-running. Mandy talks continually the whole way there.

"So, Haley, were you scared?"

"What are you talking about? Scared of what, when?"

"When Clarissa captured you and made you obey her and everything. I mean you had to have been scared right? I know I would have been. It's creepy knowing someone's capable of controlling you." Her voice changes to a slightly more ominous tone. "Right?"

At first, I'm caught a little off-guard by the question and then a thought comes across me.

"How did you know about Clarissa? How do you even know who she is?"

A nervous look comes across Mandy's face. "Uh, I—I found out about it from your dad! Yeah, when I was talking with him in the kitchen, he told me all about her."

"You already lied to me about Lana and Alex. How do I know you're telling the truth now?"

"What do you mean I lied? I didn't lie! I distinctly remember seeing Alex and Lana together!"

"Well, Lana looked me straight in the eye and told me it wasn't true!"

"Then she's a good liar because I definitely saw them together!"

I'm not getting anywhere with her. "Whatever. Let's just go shopping," I reply.

I have a hunch about what's going on with her and I'm going to need to get someone's help. Not Ethan. We're still not talking to each other. Not Lana. Right now, I don't know who to believe. There are two stories and only one can be right. That means the only person I can really talk to about Mandy is…Alex. I guess it's the only way to help her. But if I'm going to get Alex involved, he needs to know all about me.

We shop for a full two hours and we're loaded down with bags. We load it all in Mandy's car and we head back to my house. I gather my bags and say goodbye to her – all the time wondering where all this is going. She smiles at me. There's something about that smile that isn't her, but I know exactly who it reminds me of.

"Bye, Haley. Had fun shopping with you. And, um, maybe one day, you can turn me into a vampire and we can get all the vampires of the world together and rule the human race. We'd be able to drink human blood whenever we wanted. There'd be no one to call us a freak and no one to tell us what to do. Maybe I would even get powers like yours. Or even better ones! Think about it."

At that moment, that color of bright red flashes in her eyes again. What Mandy just said, and what's been happening to her eyes confirms my suspicions. As soon as she leaves, I speed to Alex's house. Before I even knock, he answers the door.

"Alex, I have a lot to tell you and I need to tell you now." I sigh. "Come with me. The forest is the best place to talk. It's the safest place to tell you what you need to hear."

He looks puzzled, but shrugs and follows. We walk the very long, familiar way because I can't show Alex that I can speed-run just yet. He needs to hear it first. We're deep in the woods when I finally say the three important words I didn't think I'd ever tell him.

"I'm a vampire."

Alex doesn't respond for a really long time until he finally says, "What are you talking about?"

We stop walking.

"I'm a vampire. I can only drink blood. I have powers that everyone else can only dream of: super-speed, super-strength, and a sonic scream. When I ran away a couple months ago, after I found out you and Lana were dating, it wasn't just because I was jealous and angry. I was sick of trying to figure out how a vampire can live a normal life. I was sick of my parents and how they were hardly ever there for me. I was just plain sick of everything. So, I left to go live with another vampire.

"She was so nice at first and her intentions seemed good, but after spending several days with her, I saw a darkness in her that I didn't want to be around. She kidnapped innocent people and expected me to kill them."

I continue to tell Alex everything – from Lana being kidnapped, to the rescue of everyone from Clarissa's headquarters, to my time with Ethan, and to the eventual killing and burying of Clarissa. Alex's jaw drops after the first few sentences and stays that way until I finish. He winces when I tell him about me pulling Clarissa's body apart. He looks as though he wants to say something, but I don't give him a chance and I continue.

"Now, Mandy has come out of nowhere trying to become my best friend. She has been acting so differently and it all started after Clarissa was buried…I think the spirit of Clarissa has possessed Mandy."

Chapter 19 - Forming a Plan

Alex just stares at me with his eyes wide open and mouth slightly agape. Then at last, he says, "Wait, so you're a vampire?

I laugh slightly. "Out of my entire speech, that's what you ask?" I pause and answer his question. "Yes, I am."

"Ok, and you killed some girl and now her spirit is inside Mandy?"

I nod sadly.

"This is kind of hard to believe."

"I swear on my life that everything I just said is true. You know me. I have never lied to you, have I?"

"Prove it to me."

I sigh. I hadn't really wanted to, but if it helps him believe me, I guess I have to. I take a couple steps back. Then I take a deep breath and I make my fangs appear. I add a little hiss just for effect.

"Whoa!" Alex yells as his arms go up in front of him as if he's defending himself.

I make my fangs disappear again and smile. "Happy?"

"You really suck blood out of things and…people?" he asks nervously.

"No!" I say quickly. I can tell that I've made him nervous. "I only suck blood out of animals unless it's someone like Clarissa who keeps trying to kill other people. I don't want to be someone who kills innocent people. I actually don't want to kill people of any kind, but I had to in her case."

"Ok, well, now that you've proved that, let's talk about Mandy. How do you know the dead person's spirit is in Mandy and how do we get it out of her?"

"Well the things Mandy has been saying -- especially today. She told me today that she wanted me to turn her into a vampire. And that once she was a vampire, we could use our combined powers to 'rule the world.' Clarissa's wanted to rule the world, and as I told you, she tried to capture my powers. Plus, on two separate occasions, I saw her eyes glow red as she spoke.

"As for how to get Clarissa's spirit out of her…I have no idea," I say with an air of hopelessness. "There is no school for vampires. You have to discover your talents and the supernatural on your own. And I know nothing about spirits. To be honest, I'm not sure who to go to for help either!"

"Ok, ok, calm down. I just have one more question. Why are you coming to me for help?"

His question takes me by surprise. I'm not exactly sure how to answer it without the moment turning into an extremely awkward one.

"Um, well, Ethan and I aren't talking right now, and I can't keep dragging Lana into potentially dangerous situations. Mom left and Dad has been getting drunk almost every night so he can ease the pain of losing her." I pause for a moment. "I guess you were really the only other person I could turn to."

Alex smiles. "Well, you seem pretty desperate, so maybe I can find someone to help us. My brother's girlfriend told us once, if I recall correctly, about a friend of hers who knew something about spirits. I'll ask her about it tonight."

"No! No one can know about me! You, Lana, and my dad are the only humans who know! I want to keep it that way!"

"Don't worry! My lips are sealed about your secret! I'll just ask her if she knows anyone who can help us with spirits, ok?"

I nod. "Ok. We can talk more tomorrow," I say. We leave the forest attempting to make light conversation, but failing miserably. Alex walks inside his door and I speed off.

When I wake up the next morning the first thought that comes to my mind is Alex. I hope he remembered to ask his brother's girlfriend for help. I'll visit him this afternoon. I get up and put a t-shirt on. I don't really feel like tying my hair up or getting dressed so I just go into the forest and drink my breakfast. I then go home and am surprised to find that Ethan is waiting in my room for me.

"Um, I'm sorry for screaming at you," he starts, quietly. "I overreacted. Can we still be boyfriend and girlfriend?"

"Listen," I say, "I accept your apology, but after what happened, I think it is best that we just stay friends."

Ethan remains silent. He gets up and leaves without saying a single word. I feel bad and I know he's sincere, but after everything that has happened between us I just don't think we could be together.

The doorbell rings. I just know it is Mandy, a.k.a. Clarissa. She has been trying to convince me to do whatever she wants and it sounds like she might even want my powers again. She has her own so why does she need mine? She most likely made up that lie about Lana and Alex so that I would stay away from them. She would have me all to herself then. She really needs to give it a rest. I run downstairs and open the door. I was right.

"Hey there! What are we going to do today? It's your call!" she says a little too bouncily. The new Clarissa is trying too hard.

"Sorry, I'm hanging out with Alex today. We've already made plans."

"Why do you want to hang out with him? I want to hang out with you!"

"Mandy, we've done things together for the past three days! Besides, we need to talk about something really important."

"Whatever. Have fun with my ex-boyfriend."

She leaves my doorstep and gets back into her car. I sigh and roll my eyes. The sooner we get Clarissa out of her, the better. I speed over to Alex's house, and for the first time he isn't the one who answers the door.

"Oh, hey!" the girl who answered the door greets me. "You must be Haley. Alex talks about you all the time! I'm Nicole!" We shake hands. "Come on in!" I step inside. A young man resembling an older Alex comes into the foyer and kisses Nicole.

"Hey there!" he says. "My name's Gabriel! As you might have guessed, I'm Alex's brother."

I smile. Gabriel has short brown hair and he's pretty tall. Nicole has long blonde hair that falls past her shoulders, and she's a little shorter than Gabriel. They both look a few years older than Alex and I. It's just then that Alex walks into the room. He looks surprised to see me. *Why? I told him I was going to talk to him today.*

"Well, I see you've met Nicole and Gabriel," he says.

"Did you ask Nicole about what we talked about?" I ask him.

"Ask me what?" Nicole answers.

I'll take that as a "no."

"Um," Alex stutters. He obviously didn't prepare what he was going to say. "Well, Nicole, do you remember that friend of yours who conducted exorcisms? See, me and Haley watched a TV show about exorcisms, and...we want to know if people like that really exist."

Nicole laughs. "I do remember talking about her. She's one of my best friends, and she definitely knows a thing or two about it. I'll see if I can get hold of her. I'll text her later tonight, ok?"

"Thanks so much Nicole! I'll stop by tomorrow," I say.

"Cool!" Nicole exclaims, as she and Gabriel leave the room with hands intertwined.

"I have a question for *you* now, Alex," I say after a pause of awkward silence. "When Nicole answered the door for me, she said you talk about me all the time. Is that true?"

His face turns bright red. "Um, I've got to go help...Gabriel set up something," he says nervously. I laugh and say goodbye.

When I get home, I look in the bathroom mirror and my face is redder than an apple! I giggle and fall onto my bed. There is a knock on my door. It's Lana. Ethan must have let her in the door.

"Where have you been? I was looking for you."

"You don't have to know where I am every second of the day, Lana."

"Well, you've run away and you were kidnapped, so, yeah, I kind of do."

"Well, if you must know, I was talking to Alex."

"Wait, what? What are you doing talking to him? I thought you two weren't talking to each other."

"You of all people should know that sometimes friends make up. And I just need his help with something."

"What 'something?' And if you need help, why aren't you coming to me for it?"

For some reason, I get really frustrated with Lana's persistence in trying to figure out everything about my life, and all of a sudden, I just blow up.

"Ok, you know what?! I need Alex's help this time and that's all you need to know. You don't have to be involved in everything that goes on!"

Lana's eyes tell me that she is deeply hurt. "I am your best friend, Haley. And you are my best friend. Best friends are supposed to be involved," she says running out of the room.

My anger drains away, and I instantly feel bad about how mean I was. I just don't want to deal with her right now. I eventually fall asleep after replaying the day's events over and over in my mind.

The next morning, I go to Alex's house as soon as I possibly can. It's Gabriel who answers the door this time.

"I was wondering when you'd show up," he laughs. "Come inside. Nicole's got something to tell you and Alex."

I step inside and Gabriel leads me to the living room. Alex is lounging on the sofa, watching T.V. Gabriel clears his throat. Alex turns.

"Hey, what's up, Haley? I thought you'd never get here!" he says teasingly.

I smile and my face starts to turn very red. *I find it amazing how Alex can still make me blush after all the heartache that he has caused me.*

"Nicole!" Gabriel calls. "Haley's here!"

Nicole walks into the room. "Hey there, Haley! I've got great news for you two!" she says, sitting down on the couch. Alex and I sit across from her. "I talked to my friend, Savanna, last night, and I told her all about you guys and how you were wondering if people like her really existed. Well, she was so excited to have someone take an interest in her, that she wants to meet the both of you as soon as she can!" Nicole explains.

Alex and I make eye contact and smile widely. *Maybe we'll get some answers,* I think.

"She said she'll try to get here as soon as possible, but she needs to clear her schedule first," Nicole continues. "She was really eager to hear about you guys. Oh, and she's bringing her friend DeLora, who is also equally experienced with exorcisms. And she also happens to be a very good friend of mine as well. They've known each other for three years and they've worked together on everything! They live in New York, and both of their schedules are crazy, so it's going to take some time before they arrive here in Virginia."

This is perfect! Maybe Clarissa is finally going away for good!

Chapter 20 - Savanna and DeLora

Two days go by before Alex texts me saying that Savanna and DeLora will arrive in a few hours at his home. As soon as I get his text, I decide to head over so we can hang out before they arrive. Once I am at his house, we decide to play video games to pass the time. Yeah, I'm not that kind of girly-girl who only cares about boys and perfect hair and make-up. I end up crushing him in *Black Ops,* but he makes me promise not to tell anyone, which makes us start laughing until our stomachs hurt. We're still trying to catch our breath and our faces are pretty red, when his doorbell rings. It's nice to hear a chime that is not my own. We both run to the door, but I let him beat me to it.

"Hi! I'm Savanna and this is my best friend, DeLora, but most people just call her Lora," the woman at the door says, shaking our hands. Savanna has short, blonde hair that comes to her shoulders, and she's a little taller than me. Lora has fine, dark brown hair and is about my height. They are absolutely beautiful.

"So, Nicole told me you were interested in removing spirits from possessed people. Is this because you just want to know about our profession, or is it because you believe someone you know is possessed?"

"We believe our friend is possessed, and we want the 'old' her back," Alex answers.

"Well, sit down, and we'll tell you everything we know and how we can get the spirit out," Savanna says. "However, we can tell you that it won't be easy."

We lead them into the living room and listen attentively.

"Well, first," Lora starts, "we must warn you that the procedure is extremely painful. One sure way to get rid of the spirit is to kill the person it is possessing because then the spirit 'dies' along with the person. But since this person is your friend, we'll rule that out and go with Option 2. Keep in mind that this process is difficult, but worth it in the end."

Savanna's voice lowers to almost a whisper. "We have a book. It's called The Book of Spirits. It's full of things to say and do for all kinds of supernatural situations. Getting spirits out of people is one of the main topics discussed, as you probably guessed from the title. But you can't tell anyone about it. There are many people who want this book for themselves and are willing to kill to get it. Anyway, the instructions are not easy to understand because it was written in Latin. So we'll help you out. Lora is much better at translating the directions than I am, and luckily we brought the book with us."

Lora runs out and gets the book from their car. She's back in a short time, carrying a book with a red, satin cover bound with a latch. The title is written in a gold script. She opens the book carefully.

"This book is hundreds of years old, so we have to be very careful with it," Savanna says. She gently opens the book. The pages are torn in several places and have yellowed over time.

"As I said before, this book is written in Latin. When performing the exorcism, you must say the words in Latin because Latin is the language of magic," Lora explains. "I'll read the first thing it says to do."

"'Position the base of your body on swards of the Earth.' Swards are defined as a turf of grass, so this means that while we perform the procedure, we need to be standing on a grassy area. The Earth's natural elements help with the exorcism.

"'Next, place the article of the spirits ten paces from the place of exorcism.' Ok, the article of the spirits is a special medallion that we have with us. The medallion helps the expulsion go easier and smoother. The spirit will go into the medallion until we get it to a place where we can keep the spirit prisoner so that it can never escape. However, if the medallion is not exactly ten paces away from your friend, the spirit will not only stay inside, it might also do something harmful to the body it is possessing.

"Lastly, you have to chant some words in Latin. I believe roughly translated, it says, 'Leave her body! You are not welcome here! Go back to where you came from and never return!' "

"How do we say those words in Latin?" Alex asks Lora.

"You must say the words perfectly, or things most likely will go wrong. I would practice a lot before actually going through with the procedure," she explains.

"The translation?" I press.

Lora takes a deep breath, as if making sure she doesn't make a mistake.

"Corpus relinquere! Non suscipiat! Exite de illa! Revertere unde orta es, et numquam rediturus!"

Alex and I stare at her. *How are we ever going to know how to say that perfectly? It sounds so complicated!* Lora and Savanna notice our faces and laugh.

"I know," Savanna says. "Latin is a difficult language. I still don't know it as well as Lora does, and I've taken it for six years! Anyway, we'll practice saying these words, and we need to prepare the site. Where's a very grassy area? It has to be green, fresh, open grass, so the procedure goes smoothly."

"Right in the middle of the nearby forest is a fairly large meadow, and the grass is really lush and green there this spring," I explain. "I go to the forest often, in case you were wondering how I know. Being a junior in high school, there's a lot of drama, so I go there and just walk around for a while. The serenity helps me feel better."

I notice a guilty look come across Alex's face. I try very hard to suppress a giggle.

"Perfect!" Savanna exclaims. "We'll practice saying the words tomorrow and prepare everything. Then on the next day, you must get your friend to come to the site willingly. If you bring her there against her will, the spirit will know what you're doing and will try to stop the exorcism."

Lora looks at her phone. "We better go now," she says. "Both of you should be here tomorrow at around three and we will practice saying those Latin words perfectly."

She and Savanna wave and leave. We hear their car starting and watch them drive away.

"You wanna watch a movie?" Alex asks me.

"Sure!" I reply.

"Awesome! You choose one, and I'll go make us some popcorn!"

While I'm looking at the huge collection of movies Alex has I'm screaming and leaping all over the place inside! I choose a mystery movie that I've wanted to see for a long time. I hold it up to Alex as he comes back from the kitchen with some buttery popcorn! My favorite! He slides the movie into the DVD player and I start eating a few kernels. Before I know it, I've eaten almost half of the bag.

About halfway through the movie, I realize that I just ate popcorn and it didn't taste disgusting. Even better, I don't feel nauseous at all! My stomach must have become accustomed to my vampire lifestyle. I don't know how it will affect me if I eat too much though, so I'll make sure to eat real food in moderation.

I start to get really tired, and soon I find that my head is resting on Alex's shoulder and his head is resting on mine. My eyes start to droop and he starts stroking my hair. *Aaahhh, dreams do come true!!* I fall asleep and miss the ending, but it doesn't matter because I had figured the mystery out anyway.

When I wake up I'm still on the couch, but Alex is gone and there's a blanket over me. I look outside and it's morning. I have just spent the whole night here.

"Good morning, sunshine!" Alex laughs as he walks into the room.

"Why didn't you wake me up so I could go home?" I ask, yawning and stretching.

"You looked so tired and I knew you needed some sleep, so I didn't want to wake you."

I smile.

"You want something to eat?" he asks.

"Oh, no, I only drink blood for meals. Usually anything other than blood tastes repulsive…."

I pause while I remember the night before.

"But last night I had my first real food, and I didn't get sick."

"Wait, so you throw up whenever you eat real food?" asks Alex.

"Remember when we went to Denny's and the movies and I had to run to the restroom twice? It's because I had eaten real food. Over time, the real food I ate started to taste really bad. I guess I'm just starting to adjust to it."

"Wow, this is all so…amazing!"

I laugh. "I'm going to go home and shower and eat, but I'll be back over here at three," I say.

"Alright! See ya then!"

I speed-run home. Just imaging Alex's expression when he sees me do this is enough to make me giggle. When I get through the door, my father is standing there with his arms folded. Uh-oh.

"Where were you, young lady?" he demands with a frown on his face.

"At a friend's. We've been talking about really important things," I answer.

"Do you have any idea how worried I was? You can't keep going away or staying out that late without calling!"

"You mean like you do?!" I scream. "You keep going out to bars and getting drunk! Do you know how much I keep worrying that one night you're not going to come back to me?!" The stern look on his face begins to fade. I continue, "Instead a policeman will come to my door and say you died in a car accident because you were driving drunk! Just because Mom's gone doesn't mean you have to endanger your life even more!"

I run up to my room, lock the door, jump out of the window, and head to the forest. I eat an animal for breakfast, and then I just walk around for a while.

After regaining my composure, I head back home, shower, and speed-run to Alex's. I see Savanna and Lora's car is already here. I ring the doorbell; Alex answers it, and pulls me in frantically.

"Is something wrong?" I ask.

Lora runs up to me.

"Someone stole the book!"

Chapter 21 - The Book

"What do you mean someone stole the book?" I ask panicky.

"Savanna and I were staying at our hotel and we left the book buried under a ton of blankets so no one could see it. We were just about ready to head over here when we looked under the blankets and the book was gone!"

"Ok, ok! Whoever stole the book must know its secrets, or know what we're planning to do," I say.

"Could it have been Clarissa?" Alex asks.

"It was Jessie," Savanna says quietly as she comes into the room.

"Who's Jessie?" he asks her.

"She's an old friend of mine. Back when we were in college, before I met Lora, Jessie and I wanted to be what Lora and I are now: professional exorcists. That's when I heard about the book. We both went crazy looking for it. Obviously, I got to it first. Jessie went psycho on me. When I asked why she wanted the book so badly, she said 'she just did.' We ceased to be friends that very minute, but not before she vowed that the book would be hers. Then she tried to drink my blood." She sighs. And after a long pause she says, "Yes, Jessie's a vampire."

Alex and I exchange glances.

"And so am I," she whispers. "I thought about it last night and decided that if I was going to be working with you, you should know."

"I'm a vampire, too," I say.

"You are?" asks Savanna with a surprised expression.

I nod.

"Lora isn't a vampire, in case you were wondering. We've just been friends for so long, and we knew so much about each other, that we just became a team. We travel everywhere helping those we can and we even opened a shop. Listen, guys, you have to get the book back from Jessie. She doesn't know how to use it properly. She can cause severe problems for herself and everyone around her."

"Well, I don't know where she could be or what she looks like. How am I supposed to find her?" I ask.

"I can speed draw a picture. Ask Lora. I'm quite the artist."

"It's true," answered Lora. "Sometimes I think her paintings are better than Leonardo da Vinci's."

Alex hands her paper and some colored pencils. She draws a perfect portrait in seconds.

"This is pretty close to what she looks like," she says when she finishes.

I examine the picture. Jessie has long, dark brown hair and brown eyes. She's gorgeous, but there's something about the picture that makes her seem unhappy, even though she's smiling.

"This is what she looked like the last time I saw her, which was about five years ago. She shouldn't have changed much," Savanna states. "You have to be careful. Jessie is dangerous. Please find her and get the book back."

I look at Alex with doubt on my face.

"You can do it, Haley," he encourages. "You've already dealt with that Clarissa chick, so Jessie will be a piece of cake."

"I'll find her," I say. I speed out of the door. I start at all of the dark places in town where a girl like her would likely hang out, but there's no sign of her.

"Haley."

It's a soft voice – barely a whisper. I can tell it isn't Clarissa's voice.

"Go back to Alex's," whispers the voice

Ok, that's really weird. I speed back to Alex's house feeling very confused; I am compelled to find out what's going on.

"It worked!" Savanna calls when she hears the door open.

"What worked?" I ask when I walk into the living room.

"Haley, you've developed the super sense of hearing! You can hear my voice from wherever you are! And you can pinpoint the location of sounds as well."

"Um, wow! Any more powers I should be aware of?"

Savanna laughs. "Most likely, no. All vampires are different, actually. I didn't think hearing would work because Alex told me that you already had speed, strength, and a sonic scream. I've only known one other vampire to have four powers, and I know quite a few vampires. It's extremely rare for us to develop more than three powers. I mean, I only have three and that's all I'm going to get."

"So the point of calling me back here was…?" I say.

"Oh, right! Alex, Lora, and I were trying to find something that might help you with your search for Jessie, and we found out that Jessie's heirloom is a necklace."

"Ok, and what the heck does a necklace have to do with anything?"

"Jessie's family is made up of vampires going back centuries," Lora explains. "When there's a long continuous line, a special heirloom is passed down from generation to generation. Jessie's heirloom is a silver necklace with a blood-red gem in the middle to symbolize her vampire heritage."

"So, how does that help me find her?"

"Not only will you now be able to look for the necklace, but we found out that the gem will glow whenever a vampire declares that they are a vampire to a human."

"So when I say 'I'm a vampire' to anyone the necklace glows?" I ask.

"Exactly. When you say that, the necklace will glow and make a small humming noise."

"So, when I confessed to Alex that I was a vampire, the necklace was glowing?"

Savanna nods. "Now, Haley, say it to Alex again and really mean it. And then concentrate on only hearing the necklace with your super hearing."

"I am a vampire," I say to Alex, meaning it with all my heart. I then close my eyes and focus on only hearing what I want. Soon, all other sounds around me fade away, and I hear a humming so soft, it just barely discernible to me. I turn my head so that both ears hear it equally well. I open my eyes and smile.

"I hear it. I know where she is," I say running out of the door. I run to the river under Parker's Bridge. What better place for a vampire to read a secret book than by a beautiful river where there is peace and quiet? I take the picture out of my pocket and hold it up. An exact match.

"I don't think that book belongs to you!" I shout to her.

Jessie looks up frantically after realizing she's not alone anymore.

"Leave me alone!" she screams at me.

"Give me the book!" I reply just as loudly.

She tries to run away, but she doesn't have super-speed like I do. I catch up to her easily, and accidently push her into a tree once I catch her. Thankfully, she has super-strength, so she's not hurt, just dazed. I take the book from her and smile.

"I'll take that," I say.

"Wait," she says softly, her eyes starting to water. "You don't understand."

"I understand that you took something that doesn't belong to you!"

"I didn't want to, but I had to."

"You didn't have to. You had a choice."

"No, I didn't. It's tradition in my family that when you turn ten years old, you must locate the Book of Spirits, and do whatever is necessary to get it. Well, as soon as I turned ten, I began my search. I searched all day, every day and I never found it. I didn't celebrate my tenth birthday like a normal girl. Ever since that day my parents have looked at me like I was the biggest mistake they ever made. I had shamed them. They stopped loving me, and they didn't care about me. They never will care about me again until I find the book. I have never stopped searching." She begins to sob. "I just wanted to be loved!"

"So, since your parents are vampires, is that how you got the necklace?"

"Yeah, they gave me this when I was a baby. It has to be passed down from generation to generation. It's my responsibility to make sure that it continues. I can never take it off until it's time to give it to the next generation."

"Why do you keep something that helps vampires track you?"

"I don't know. It was designed by my ancestors. I guess they were only thinking of relatives finding them, not strangers."

"Why don't you just keep it in a safe place and not wear it?"

"If I don't wear it my parents will be even more ashamed than they already are. When the gem lights up I know someone could be looking for me. So I usually have time to get away. Only vampires hear the hum, since it's a vampire charm. And the vampire must have super hearing in order to find me which is quite rare among vampires."

"Savanna told me you tried to drink her blood to get that book."

"I only wanted to show my parents that I had found the book, but she didn't understand. I just wanted to drink enough blood to knock her unconsciousness for an hour or so, but she thought I was trying to kill her."

I feel so bad for Jessie. Savanna made it sound like she was a cold-blooded killer, when all she wanted was to feel love and affection from her parents. "Please," I start, "I don't care what you do with the book later, but I need it right now. My friend is possessed by the spirit of an evil vampire. Savanna, Lora, and my friend Alex are trying to help. Just let me get the spirit out."

"Would the evil vampire's name happen to be Clarissa?"

Faith Miller

"Yes! How did you know?"

"Clarissa may seem very nice at first, but she has a thirst for blood and power that she can't control. I met her when I was just turning 13. She knew everything that was going on and convinced me to work with her."

"That's exactly what happened to me. I drank all her blood, ripped her body apart, and buried her. Unfortunately, her spirit came back and is possessing one of my best friends."

"Then you must be pretty special because Clarissa has never tried so hard to keep one of us. You have to get Clarissa out of your friend. She can cause really serious damage." She wipes her cheeks. "You can have the book. But please, at least let me show it to my parents so they will know I'm not a failure."

"I'll try to talk to Savanna about it. Or possibly, you can."

"No! She won't listen to me. She doesn't understand me!"

"But she will if you get her to listen. Just try."

"I will…"

I give her a hopeful look and speed off. When I open the door to Alex's, Savanna runs to me faster than I thought she could.

"Did you get the book back?" she asks fervently.

I hand her the book and she grabs it carefully as if it's the first time she's ever laid hands on it. We go back to the living room and as soon as Alex sees the book, he runs up and hugs me.

"I knew you could do it!" he says.

I scream incredibly loud inside, letting out a soft giggle on the outside, and pull him along so we can practice the Latin words. *It's already seven o'clock and we were supposed to start at three. Where did the time go? The site has to be prepared tonight. We cannot afford to wait another day.* For the next hour, Alex and I practice saying what we must say for tomorrow.

"Now," Lora says when we've finally got the chant down correctly, "we must go prepare the site."

Savanna goes to her car and gets the medallion, or item of the spirits as it is known. It is made of pure gold and has a brilliant blue gem in the center. We take the medallion and the book with us as we all head to the big meadow in the center of the forest. The grass is a lush green.

After some group discussion, we decide where Mandy will be when we perform the exorcism. Savanna puts an unusual rock we find on the grass to mark the spot. She then measures exactly ten paces away from where Mandy will stand and places the medallion on the grass there.

"If this medallion is moved at all, the exorcism will not work. Make sure it stays exactly where it is," Lora says. Everything is in place, Alex and I know the chant and we've prepared the site. We're ready.

"Get your friend to come here at exactly twelve in the afternoon. Exorcisms work best when the sun is at its highest point."

She sighs.

"Is something wrong?" I ask.

"We're taking a risk. At this point, the spirit has possessed the body for so long that getting it out might take longer and be more painful. I'm not saying it won't come out, but the results might be different than for a person who has only been possessed for about a day," Lora explains. "Keep in mind that she might not be the same person she was before she was possessed."

Alex and I exchange a glance.

This will work...won't it?

Chapter 22 - Performing the Exorcism

It's dark outside when I walk into the door of my house. I am a little afraid that Dad will be standing there yelling at me again since it's so late, but instead Ethan and Lana ambush me. *Why isn't Lana ever at her own house? She doesn't sleep here, but she's just always here! Is there something going on with Ethan and her that I don't know about?*

"Haley, we need to talk," she says, pulling me to the sofa. She pushes me down and they both sit across from me.

"You've been avoiding us," Ethan says.

"What are you talking about?" I protest.

"You're gone all the time!" Lana cries. "You haven't talked to either of us in forever! What's going on?"

Why can't they just mind their own business? The pressures of the day have been too much for me and I explode.

"Listen, I'm tired and I don't feel like discussing anything right now!" I yell. "I'm asking you two to mind your own beeswax! I'll talk to you when I'm ready!"

I run up to my room and lock the door. I immediately feel like I'm doing that too much lately. I lie in bed, wishing I lived alone.

The next morning, I wake up and check the clock beside my bed. It's 10 o'clock! I overslept! I get quickly get dressed, grab my cell, and text Mandy to meet me at my house at 11:30. She asks me what we're going to do. I say that we are going to take a walk in the woods, adding that we'll go shopping later since just going to the woods didn't sound like the most fun thing to do. I hop out the window. If I go out the front door I'll have to pass Ethan, and that's an awkward moment waiting to happen. Mandy pulls up and we start walking into the woods. I glance at my phone and see its 11:45. Perfect. Just enough time to get her to the site.

"So, remind me why we're in the woods," Mandy says.

"It's so peaceful in here, and I thought it'd be a nice place to just walk and talk for a while. We never seem to do that anymore," I reply.

We walk slowly and make casual conversation until we arrive at the meadow at the center of the woods. Savanna and Lora are standing there. Out of the corner of my eye, I see Alex peek out from behind a tree at the edge of the meadow. He's holding the Book of Spirits.

"Who are they?" Mandy asks, almost like she's irritated. Clarissa wanted me alone, I bet.

"Oh, they're just people who take care of the forest. They clean up litter, make sure there's nothing harmful in here, keeping everything and everyone safe.

Stuff like that," I lie. I walk around, until I have Mandy standing next to the rock we had placed earlier.

Alex runs swiftly from behind the tree and we quickly stand together and hold the book.

"What are you doing?" Mandy asks frantically.

"Getting rid of you Clarissa!" I scream.

"Nooo!" she yells, stepping forward to stop us.

"Corpus relinqure! Non suscipiat!" Alex and I chant. Mandy steps back next to the rock and starts screaming. It hurts me to see her like that, but it must be done.

"Exite de illa!"

At this point, Mandy starts gagging and something starts coming out of her mouth. It's Clarissa's spirit.

"Revertere unde orta es, et numquam rediturus!" we finish.

The spirit comes out fully, leaving Mandy collapsed on the ground and unconscious.

Clarissa's spirit looms in the air, then it slowly morphs into someone else. The spirit of the true person it represents. I can't believe it…

"Mom?" I ask quietly.

"I'm sorry, Haley," she says.

"Why did you do this? Why did you kill so many people? Why did you do this to me?"

"I trained you to control your thirst for blood, but I didn't have anyone to train me. It started off with only two people a week. Then, as I got older, the desire for blood became stronger. I couldn't control it anymore and had to leave so I wouldn't hurt you or your father. Soon, the need for human blood was so strong that it completely changed my entire personality. I wasn't myself anymore. I had become Clarissa and I needed to do everything in my power to acquire human blood and stay in control. As long as I was the most powerful vampire, I would have all the human blood I would ever need. I needed your powers to ensure I was the most powerful."

The spirit holds her arms out to me and I walk toward her.

Savanna chants additional words in Latin that I don't understand and the spirit is sucked into the medallion.

"Mom," I whisper.

I sink down and to cry softly. My mom hadn't been there for me for a long time, but the thought of her gone forever was unimaginable.

Alex rubs my shoulder and I look up and still see Mandy on the ground. Lora and Savanna are kneeling next to her. I get up, trying to focus more on the task at hand, and Alex and I rush over to Mandy. Her chest is rising up and down, so I know she's alive.

"It may be some time before she wakes up," Lora says, breaking the silence. "Like I said last night, the spirit has inhabited the body for so long, I don't know if she'll ever be the same."

"I've got to get her to my house," I say. I pick her up as gently as I can and speed her to my house, being extremely careful not to hurt her. I bang my foot on the door and Lana opens it. Like I said before, why is she never at her own house? It's okay. I need her right now.

"Oh, my gosh," she exclaims.

I carry Mandy up the stairs and into my room and place her on my bed. Lana comes in behind me.

"This is what I've been doing," I say without turning. "Mandy was possessed by the spirit of Clarissa and I had to get her out. She was slowly killing Mandy. I guess I went to Alex for help because I wanted an excuse to be with him and talk to him. I think even after everything that has happened I still had feelings for him."

I hear Lana sigh as if she understands. I turn to her. "My mom was Clarissa."

"What?"

"The reason Mom left home was to become Clarissa forever. She couldn't be around Dad and me anymore because of her inability to control her thirst for human blood. I'm sorry I got mad at you. It's just that I had a perfect night with Alex and I was mad that I had to come back to reality."

Mandy stirs. Lana runs to the bedside.

"Where am I?" she whispers hoarsely.

"You're in my room," I answer. "Do you remember anything?"

"I remember walking through the woods because I had to write a report about Ralph Waldo Emerson for English class. I thought being outdoors would help me think. Then there was a really strange whispering noise, and... I woke up here. Everything in between is just a big blur."

"Mandy, you were possessed by the spirit of an evil vampire whom I killed. She killed so many people. I was able to destroy her because I'm a vampire too."

Mandy then says something I didn't expect her to say. "I know."

"How'd you find out?" I ask incredulously.

"I saw you killing and drinking the blood from an animal in the woods a couple weeks ago. It really scared me but I didn't want to scare anyone else by telling them about what I saw so I kept it to myself. You're one of my best friends. I couldn't take the chance that you would be harmed if others found out about you."

I smile at Mandy's kindness.

"My throat's sore," she says as she begins to rub it with her hand.

"It was rough getting the spirit out. I'll go get you some water." I speed out and bring her a glass of water from my bathroom. Mandy sips it slowly. I continue to tell Mandy all about Clarissa and everything about my vampire life.

"You need to rest," I say when I finish explaining everything to her. "You've been through a lot. Stay in my bed and I'll call your mom. I don't want you getting up for a while."

"But this is your bed. I don't want to take it."

"I don't mind. You need it more than I do. I'll call your parents and let them know you're just going to spend the night here."

Mandy sighs and closes her eyes. She's so sore, she can't turn over. I feel bad for her. She didn't do anything to deserve this. Lana and I leave, as I close the door behind me.

It's over.

Chapter 23 - Couples

Lana and I need to let Mandy rest so we walk down the hall quietly.

We walk downstairs to find Ethan sitting on the couch.

"Ethan," I start, "I'm so sorry for yelling at you. I just had so much on my mind and I was a little overwhelmed."

"It's alright," he says. "I'm sorry I kept adding to your stress."

We hug, silently forgiving each other.

"Ethan, you're a vampire," I say, realizing something.

"Thanks for noticing," he laughs.

"Well, when Clarissa came back for me the second time, she said I'm not like other vampires. And when I talked to this another vampire who knew Clarissa, she said that I must be special if Clarissa was trying that hard to get to me. Do you know what they were talking about?"

"Actually, believe it or not, I do. You have four powers, Haley. Most vampires only have two or three. You are also surrounded with affection. You have a father who loves you very much and you have so many great friends who care about you even though you are a vampire. Most vampires don't have that. They're shunned by everyone they have ever known because they are different. And you're not like that. That's why you are different from all other vampires. The love shown toward you reaches your heart and it projects out to everyone you meet. It makes you a more powerful vampire. Clarissa wanted you so badly because you were becoming more powerful than her and it was eating her alive. She tried to take your powers so that she would be supreme once again."

It's hard to believe that my own mother was really capable of all that.

Lana clears her throat breaking the silence. We both look at her.

"Oh, right!" Ethan exclaims suddenly, as if he just remembered something, which he probably did. "Haley, there's something we need to tell you." He puts his arm around Lana's shoulders and her arm goes around his waist. *No way!*

"We've started dating!" Lana exclaims.

"Wow, when did this happen?" I ask happily.

"Well, when you were gone all the time, we were usually the only two in the house and who else were we going to talk to? We talked about you a lot at first, I'll admit. But the more we talked, the more we realized how much we had in common and it just… happened."

"Oh my gosh, guys! I'm so happy for you two!" I exclaim, hugging them both. "Well, I've gotta go explain things to my dad and hopefully get some explanations back. Congratulations!"

I run upstairs to Dad's room. He's putting away some of his clothes.

"Haley," he says when he sees me, "we need to talk."

"I know. Dad, why didn't you tell me about Mom? You said that the last vampire in her family was killed long ago. And why didn't you tell me the real reason she left?"

"I thought that it would be hard for you to learn that your mother had become a killer. I didn't think you could handle the truth. Haley, you don't know the whole story either. Your mother never actually got drunk. Whenever we stayed out late, I was getting drunk. She was going out and killing people for their blood. By the time she started, though, I was so drunk I didn't even care. It's been that way for years and years. I'm so sorry I didn't tell you. I also wanted to protect you from her, so I sent someone to watch out for you and keep her away from you. I sent the protector to you and he did his job. He helped you escape when you had been kidnapped and I'm thankful. He wasn't allowed to interfere with family affairs, which is why he couldn't keep you from meeting and battling your mother, or as you knew her, Clarissa. I just wish you hadn't had to find out about your mother that way."

"I'm really sorry about yelling at you and for what I said. It's just that everything was starting to go great for me, for the most part, and I was just afraid that at any moment it was all going to be ruined. I mean,

Alex and I were finally bonding, I ate some real food for the first time in weeks, and it was just perfect."

"No, I'm the one who should be apologizing. I should have told you the truth, but it was just too hard to believe that it was really happening. And I've been thinking about what you said and you're right. I had no idea you felt that way. It was selfish of me not to think of how you were affected by my drinking. It's not fair to you that I let you worry about me at your age. You're supposed to be out with friends and having fun. But instead, all you can think about is my safety. So, I'm going to try to stop drinking...for you. You can't lose another parent."

I smile and we hug tightly.

"Go on," he says. "Go have fun with your friends. Like Alex," he winks at me. "I'll be right here."

"Thanks, Dad. I'm glad you're going to stop drinking. It's better for you more than it is me."

I speed over to Alex's house once more to see Savanna and Lora off. When I ring the doorbell, Savanna is the one who answers.

"Hey there! I was hoping you'd stop by so we could say our proper good-byes."

I laugh and step inside.

"I can't thank you enough for all your help," I tell the two women. "Mandy's pretty sore, but she's going to be just fine."

"I'm glad we could help," Savanna says. "And about Jessie--I've decided to let her join us in our profession and give her total possession of the book. The book is rightfully hers."

"You're doing the right thing. There are some things about Jessie that you don't know, and once she tells you the real reason she wanted the book, you'll understand."

Gabriel, Nicole, and Alex come up to the door. Savanna, Lora, and Nicole all hug.

"It was great to see you guys again," Nicole says.

"You too, Nicole," Lora answers. "If you ever need our help, you know where to reach us!"

"New York City Exorcism Shop!" she laughs.

"Well, we better get going. "

Savanna and Lora step out, get into their car, and drive away.

"Nicole, thank you so much for getting them to come here," I say.

"Oh, it was no problem! I'm just glad I could help. They sure stayed here a long time just to explain their profession," she says curiously.

"Well, it was more than just knowing about their profession," I say. "There was…more to it."

"Whatever you say!" Nicole laughs.

She and Gabriel go into another room, so it's just me and Alex. We walk to the couches in the living room.

"How's Mandy doing?" he asks.

"Pretty rough. Her throat's sore and she's really achy, but she's still the same Mandy! Clarissa just wasn't strong enough to rid Mandy of her kindness."

"That's great! I'm sorry that you had to find out about your mom that way. No one deserves that. But I'm really glad you told me about all of the things that were going on with Mandy, and everything about you. It really clears up a lot of things that happened in the past," he says.

"Well, I felt that since you and Mandy had dated, you had a right to know what was going on."

We start to draw closer to each other. Our eyes close. The kiss that we share sends me flying into another world where it's just Alex and me. It's my first kiss with him that I have so long awaited. Then Alex says the four words I've wanted to hear from him ever since I got to know him.

"I love you, Haley."

"I love you too."

There's a pause.

"Are you ok dating a vampire?" I ask him.

"I look past that fact and look into your heart. And in your heart, you're the girl I want to be with, vampire or not. You're an amazing girl, Haley. After all you've been through, I truly see how strong you are. You have faced more struggles than anyone I have ever known and you got through them all. You continue to amaze me and I just want to be with you."

I giggle. "I've got to tell Lana this. After all, don't you think she has a right to know, since she's my best friend and has wanted this to happen as long as I have?"

"You're right. She does deserve to know. But if you're going to go tell her, I'm going with you."

We walk out of the door, hands intertwined. I walk into my house and call Lana's name. She and Ethan walk to the door. When she sees me, she grins, because she knows what's happened before I even say the words.

"Lana, Ethan, you two may have started dating, but I've also got someone to be with now. Alex and I are now dating," I say.

Lana and I squeal and do our happy hug. I feel slightly embarrassed, but we continue to hug anyway. Ethan and Alex smile at us.

That night, we go on a double date. I have Dad watch over Mandy and make sure she's okay while we're gone. Ethan and I eat from a couple animals in the woods before we leave, even though we both believe we can eat normal food now. But I don't know how much normal food I can eat without getting sick, and I don't want a repeat of the movie theater experience. The four of us decide to have dinner at The Melting Pot. Ethan and I only eat the chocolate fondue, since that's the best part and since we already had "dinner." When we're about to separate, Alex and I share another kiss, and Ethan and Lana share one of their own. Alex drops me off at my house leaving me feeling the happiest I have felt in a long time. Mandy continues to sleep in my bed, so I sleep on the couch downstairs.

The next morning, Mandy has almost made a full recovery. I bring her breakfast in bed, and she thanks me endlessly. By the afternoon, Mandy's ready to go home.

"Thank you so much for helping me, Haley," she says.

"I'm just glad you're okay. Um, Mandy, you might not like this, but I want you to hear it from me before you hear it anywhere else. I'm kind of dating Alex now."

She laughs. "I knew it would happen sooner or later. I saw the way he looked at you and the way you looked at him. But it's okay. I'm not mad. I just keep it in perspective. I've had two years with him and we fought a lot. We may not have shown it in public, but we did. While I wanted to deny it while we were dating, I knew that you were better for him. After we broke up, I realized he was not the guy for me. So, I'm just going to wait until the right one comes along." She then says very sincerely to me with a smile, "I hope you two are happy."

I don't think Mandy could get any nicer if she tried. We hug again and I see her out the door. A couple hours later, Alex shows up at my door and greets me with a hug and a kiss. My mind flashes back to the time when I saw him do this with Mandy. I blush when I think about how he does it with me now.

"I'm sorry about all the hurt I've caused you," he apologizes.

"It was worth it to be where we are now."

"I love you."

"I love you more."

We kiss again.

For the first time since I found out I was a vampire, everything's just right.

No, everything's perfect.

Upcoming Books and Information

Not Myself is the first novel written by 17 year old author Faith Miller. Go to www.deepseapublishing.com for more information on Faith and her upcoming book events.

If you like this story, you'll also enjoy:

- *Let Sleeping Dragons Lie*, by Tryone Burson
- *Hardt's Tale*, by Gwendolyn Druyor
- *The Good Fight*, by Ophelia Hu
- *The Gallivan Legacy*, by Sable Lewis
- *The Bryant Family Chronicles*, by Eddie Hughes
- *Capria Rodalia*, by Sidney McPhail

Like *Not Myself*, these award winning works are available in paperback and eBook form at Deep Sea Publishing's Online Store, BarnesAndNoble.com, Amazon, and Apple's iBookstore. The website also lists the shops and bookstores that carry the books. These books can be ordered from any bookstore as well using the ISBN.

Deep Sea Publishing (DSP) is a Florida-based company publishing fictional novels, young adult/teen fiction, children's books, photography books, and reference guides.

Made in the USA
Lexington, KY
14 June 2013